**"Here, let me check the house first."
Jack leaped ahead of her up the
concrete steps of her small porch.
"I'll take a look around inside, just to
be on the safe side."**

Susanna followed him in and stood, hugging little
Lizzie tight while Jack made a tour through her small
home. The alarm created by the detective's warning
was fading. She would feel much safer now, knowing
a killer wasn't waiting to jump out at her the moment
she and Lizzie were alone.

Jack reappeared in the living room. "Everything's
fine. I made sure all the windows were locked, too."

"Thank you." She forced herself to smile. This guy
was certainly an anomaly. One minute he offended
her, and the next he was going the extra mile to
make sure she felt safe. "I appreciate that."

The moment he left, a wave of anxiety threatened
her composure. *What if the detective was right?
What if someone is watching, waiting to get me
alone?*

Books by Virginia Smith

Love Inspired Suspense

Murder by Mushroom
Bluegrass Peril
A Taste of Murder
Murder at Eagle Summit
Scent of Murder
Into the Deep
A Deadly Game

Love Inspired

A Daughter's Legacy

VIRGINIA SMITH

A lifelong lover of books, Virginia Smith has always enjoyed immersing herself in fiction. In her mid-twenties she wrote her first story and discovered that writing well is harder than it looks; it took many years to produce a book worthy of publication. During the daylight hours, she steadily climbed the corporate ladder and stole time to write late at night after the kids were in bed. With the publication of her first novel, she left her twenty-year corporate profession to devote her energy to her passion—writing stories that honor God and bring a smile to the faces of her readers. When she isn't writing, Ginny and her husband, Ted, enjoy exploring the extremes of nature—skiing in the mountains of Utah, motorcycle riding on the curvy roads of central Kentucky and scuba diving in the warm waters of the Caribbean. Visit her online at www.VirginiaSmith.org.

A
DEADLY
GAME

VIRGINIA SMITH

Steeple
Hill®

Published by Steeple Hill Books™

STEEPLE HILL BOOKS

Steeple
Hill®

Recycling programs
for this product may
not exist in your area.

ISBN-13: 978-0-373-44428-1

A DEADLY GAME

www.SteepleHill.com

Printed in U.S.A.

Ask and it will be given to you; seek and you will find; knock and the door will be opened to you.
—*Matthew* 7:7, NIV

For my son, Jonathan Leake.
As you seek to solve your own mysteries,
don't forget that the answers
are already written down.

Acknowledgments

Thanks so much to my husband, Ted, for patiently answering questions about cars and auctions and dirt bikes. I'm grateful to my sister, Susie Smith, who helped me figure out where to hide tokens all over Central Kentucky. Huge thanks to my editor, Tina James, for brainstorming above and beyond the call of duty. I'm grateful to Wendy Lawton for a million things. And of course my undying gratitude goes to my Lord, Who knows all mysteries and reveals all things hidden.

PROLOGUE

Rich men died just as easily as poor men. As he looked down at the body before his feet, that fact disturbed the killer even more than the act he'd just committed. In the end, money bought no advantage. The wealthy, too, fell victim to the great equalizer of men—death.

Killer. A shudder rippled through his frame at the word. That was how he must now think of himself. He'd sunk to a new low, performed an act he had not considered himself capable of. Murder.

A fleeting wave of regret passed through him, but he dismissed it impatiently and returned his weapon, a computer laptop cord, to its place on the credenza. He'd had no choice. The man's death was his own fault. He could have cooperated, made them both some money. Instead, he'd resorted to threats. Well, this was one rich man who would never threaten to expose anyone again, would he?

The killer glanced at his watch. Not much time. If he were caught here, everything would fall apart. They'd convict him of a whole list of crimes, a list that started with murder. Even if the police didn't catch him, there were others who would, and he feared them even more. He may yet end up as dead as his victim. Adrenaline and fear in equal measures coursed through his body and his gaze slid around the office. So many possible hiding places. Where to start?

Ten minutes later, he could no longer ignore the compelling urge to flee. He hadn't found a thing. But he wasn't ready to give up yet, not by a long shot.

He let himself out of the office and hurried to the secretary's desk out front. A quick search of the drawers paid off. From a file labeled *Personal Receipts* in neat block letters, he extracted a cell phone bill and copied down the name, address and phone number printed at the top. Then he slid the file back in place and closed the drawer. Two smiling faces peered into his from a framed photograph on the corner of the desk, a young woman and a child with golden curls.

A smile crept across his lips as he committed the faces to memory.

ONE

The moment she rounded the corner of the building, Susanna Trent knew something was wrong. To her right, darkness shrouded the wooded area that ran the length of the building housing Ingram Industries. Tiny frozen daggers of sleet sliced through the nighttime sky to fall onto the crowded evergreen branches, the contact goading the trees into an eerie dance. To her left, slivers of light peeked through the cracks of closed blinds in the floor-to-ceiling office windows. Sleet stung her cheeks and slapped at the nylon hood of her jacket as she skidded to a halt on the sidewalk.

Behind her, Jack Townsend didn't stop quite as quickly. He bumped into her, and almost knocked her off her feet.

Jack slipped a strong hand under her arm to steady her. "Sorry about that."

Susanna acknowledged the apology with an absent nod, her stare fixed on the windows. A finger of disquiet tapped at the edges of her mind. She'd expected to see her boss standing there, waiting for her to arrive with his new Corvette. Mr. Ingram had been ecstatic when she called him after the auction ended to tell him that she'd succeeded in buying the car he wanted. Why wasn't he watching for the moment she arrived, ready to dash outside to see it? Something definitely wasn't right here.

Jack's head turned as he followed her gaze. "Is something wrong?"

Susanna shook her head, as much to dislodge the uneasy feelings as to answer. "It's just that the blinds are closed. They're never closed."

"Maybe he wanted some privacy."

"From what?" She pointed toward the desolate woods. "Nobody ever comes back here except him and me."

Jack peered into the ice-covered evergreens, then shrugged. "Why don't we ask him?"

His smile tilted sideways, and Susanna couldn't help but admire the guy's strong jaw, chiseled nose and short-cropped dark hair. They'd just met a few hours ago, at the car auction, and she'd noted his wholesome good looks right off. Normally she would have found him attractive, but Jack Townsend was exactly the kind of man she made a point of avoiding. He shared too much in common with someone she hoped she'd never have to see again.

Still, he was doing Mr. Ingram a favor by delivering the new Corvette. She had to admit that was a nice gesture, especially when he had been bidding against her for the same car. Unusual, too. In Susanna's experience, the sons of billionaires were far too self-centered to do something nice for someone else.

She glanced again at the closed blinds and couldn't completely dismiss the feeling of foreboding that bloomed. Hurrying to the heavy metal door, she shrugged the strap of her voluminous handbag from her shoulder. The cavernous interior of the purse held a wealth of useful personal items, with plenty of room for the envelope containing the papers for Mr. Ingram's new car. But it also ate keys. She rummaged inside, shaking to listen for the telltale jingle. Finally, she found them. Her gloved fingers fumbled to locate the right one, and she shoved it into the lock.

The hallway inside was empty, but it would be at this time of night. Susanna led Jack down the short corridor and around the corner. A quick glance toward the front of the building showed that the main lights were off in the accounting department. Stillness filled the office, normally bustling in the daytime. A few safety lights cast a dim glow over the empty desks.

She didn't pause when she entered her own work space, but hurried across the carpeted floor, past her tidy desk. The door to Mr. Ingram's private office had been pulled almost closed. Was he on a phone call, maybe? She halted for a moment, but didn't hear any noise from inside.

"Mr. Ingram?" She tapped on the wood, the sound muted by her gloves. "I'm here with your car."

No answer. Alarm crept like spider legs up the back of Susanna's neck. Something was wrong; she could feel it. She exchanged a glance with Jack, whose brows had drawn together over eyes dark with concern.

"Mr. Ingram? Is everything okay?"

Susanna laid a gloved hand on the solid door and gave a gentle push. It swung inward, and she slipped through the enlarged opening. The desk chair was empty, but her gaze was drawn to the floor.

A body lay halfway hidden behind the big wooden desk. But the head was visible. The image seared into Susanna's brain like a hot brand, and she knew she would remember it as long as she lived. Mr. Ingram's face was purple, his eyes bulging from their sockets to stare at something no living person could see.

A scream tore from her throat.

While the police officer took his statement, Jack tried not to look toward Ingram's open office door. From the corner of his eye he saw a flash from the investigator's camera as it photographed the body. He suppressed a shudder and glanced in the opposite direction, where Susanna sat huddled in a chair, her face hidden behind a curtain of blond hair. The horrified sound of her scream still echoed in his ears. She spoke quietly into a cell phone, which she held cupped to the side of her head with one hand while she massaged her temples with the thumb and forefinger of the other. Something about the way her drooping shoulders gave an occasional heave, as if she was holding back sobs, made Jack want to cross the room and place a comforting arm around her.

The thought brought a sour taste to his mouth. An offer of compassion might be viewed as an invitation, and he wasn't about to get himself any more involved with Susanna Trent than he already was. They'd known each other only a few hours, and already the gruesome specter of a dead body had polluted any budding relationship they might have enjoyed. That, and the fact that she knew who he was. The name Townsend cast a long shadow in Lexington, Kentucky.

"Thank you for answering our questions, Mr. Townsend." Jack pulled his attention away from Susanna and focused on the police detective. The man, who had identified himself as Detective Rollins, gave a quick smile. "If you don't mind, we'd like to get an address and phone number where we can reach you in case something comes up that we need to clarify."

"Of course." Jack slid his wallet out of his jeans pocket and extracted a card.

Rollins took it out of his hand and studied it. "Vice President of Supply for Townsend Steakhouses, Inc." The detective didn't bother to hide the fact that he was impressed. "That sounds like an important job."

"Yes, it certainly does." Jack worded his answer carefully, and hoped his smile was sincere.

The detective's expression turned quizzical, but he didn't pursue the matter. "Well, we may be in touch. In the meantime, if you think of anything that could be helpful, give us a call."

Rollins handed the card to the uniformed officer standing next to him, who began copying information from it. With another quick smile, this time in dismissal, the detective headed for Ingram's office.

Apparently Jack was free to leave. He glanced toward Susanna, who had not moved from her chair and was still speaking quietly into her phone. Hopefully she was talking to someone who would offer her the support she needed. A boyfriend, maybe. Though he felt a twinge of guilt at leaving her to face the detective's questions alone, he had his own call to make. He'd put it off long enough.

Jack extracted his cell phone from his pocket and pressed the power button as he stepped from the building into the cold evening air. He hurried down the sidewalk toward his truck, which still had the big covered car trailer hitched to the back. The sleet had stopped for the moment, but his breath froze in visible puffs as he scrolled down the listings in his cell phone address book to the entry for his father, R. H. Townsend. When Jack came to work in the office of Townsend Steakhouses, his father had insisted that he stop being childish and address him as R.H., like all the other management employees. In Jack's mind, he'd been R.H. for years anyway. Giving that cold man the title Father had felt wrong for a long time.

The time read just past nine, which meant that R.H. would be in his home office, working for several more hours before he went to bed. Jack pictured him behind his desk, reading from a neat stack of papers, jotting notes on the yellow legal pad he kept nearby at all times to record the not-infrequent ideas that kept the research and development department at Townsend Steakhouses in a perpetual state of flustered activity.

The phone didn't finish the first ring.

"I've been trying to call you for hours. Did you get the car?" No greeting. R. H. Townsend rarely wasted time on pleasantries.

"I'm afraid not. The b—"

"What?"

A string of foul language polluted the airspace between Jack's phone and his father's. Jack set his teeth together and endured the tirade. If the frigid air had turned blue around him, he wouldn't have been surprised. His father's language was rarely appropriate for Sunday school, but this outburst went on longer than usual.

When he paused for a breath, Jack jumped in to defend himself. "Wait a minute. If you'll just listen—"

"Listen? That's what I expected you to do—listen to me, and do as you were told. But I guess it was asking too much to expect you to follow one simple request."

The scorn in his father's words was all too familiar. It was a tone Jack had heard many times since his boyhood.

"Who bought it?"

Jack squeezed his eyes shut before he said the name. "Tom Ingram's secretary."

"You let a *secretary* buy my car out from under your nose?"

Another tirade followed, and Jack let it run dry before he offered his explanation. "The car sold for thirty thousand dollars. I checked a whole list of comparables before I left for the auction, so I know that's more than it was worth.

But I located another red Corvette up near Indianapolis, and it's in even b—"

"Just forget it. I don't want to hear your excuses."

With iron control, Jack bit back the words that threatened to shoot out of his mouth. His chest expanded slowly as he drew icy air into his lungs. He'd long ago given up trying to defend his actions to his father.

Besides, he had another blow to deliver, and there was no way to soften it. His father and Thomas Ingram had been friends.

Jack kept his tone even as he spoke. "R.H., I have something to tell you that may come as a shock." He drew another breath, then broke the news. "Tom Ingram is dead."

"Dead? Don't tell me he wrecked the car as soon as he got it."

Jack arrived at the pickup, and unlocked the door with a click of the remote. "No, it wasn't an accident. He was killed. Murdered, right in his office."

Silence on the line. Jack opened the door and climbed into the driver's seat. A trace of warmth still lingered in the cab from his ninety-minute drive after the auction. He pictured his father, seated in his high-backed chair, digesting the news. He and Ingram were among a small group of wealthy businessmen who'd been in the habit of getting together for a monthly poker game for the past several years. Ingram's death would be a blow to them all.

"That's…terrible. Just terrible. Where did you hear about it? Is it on the radio?"

"No, I don't think the press has gotten wind of the news yet. After his secretary bought the car, she couldn't find a transport company to deliver it tonight. They were all booked solid for several days. Since I had taken an empty trailer with me anyway, I offered to bring the Corvette back to Lexington for her. We found the body when we got here."

"Wait a minute. First you let someone else buy my car, and then you *delivered* it for her?"

Jack stiffened at the outrage in his father's voice. "Maybe you didn't hear me. I just told you that your friend has been killed—murdered—and I found the body. And all you can think about is a car?"

"I said it was terrible. What more do you want me to say?" Jack heard a quick intake of breath. "What's going to happen to the car now? Ingram certainly doesn't need it anymore."

He shook his head, unable to answer for a moment. Obviously he'd been wrong to describe Ingram as his father's friend. R.H. had no friends. He had social acquaintances, business associates and employees, but certainly no one in whom he would confide as a friend. Jack had heard the lecture many times growing up—confidences were an act of weakness. Why would you tell someone your thoughts and give them a weapon that might be used against you later? Being too open with people was one of the many things for which R. H. Townsend faulted his son.

Still, a man had been murdered. Jack had known his father rarely wasted time on sentimentality, but to express an interest in the Corvette this soon? It was downright callous.

If that's what being a successful businessman leads to, Lord, then save me from success.

There was no use trying to convince his father that the question was inappropriate. The man was a brusque, uncaring businessman through and through, and he wasn't likely to change his attitude anytime soon.

Jack finally managed an even response. "I overheard his secretary tell the police that Ingram has two daughters.

The car probably belongs to them now. Maybe they'd be willing to sell it to you."

"How long do you think that would take?"

Jack closed his eyes. "I really don't know."

"Check on it then."

A click, and the call disconnected. For a long time, Jack sat staring at the phone. He'd seen his father make some harsh business decisions with little regard for the people whose lives he had affected. He'd watched him sign away the jobs and livelihood of hundreds of employees with the flourish of a pen, without even a passing thought to their welfare. Heard him more than once berate midlevel managers with language that should have resulted in lawsuits. And he'd been on the receiving end of that famous Townsend temper more times than he could count. He thought nothing the man could do would surprise him anymore. But this reaction to Tom Ingram's death plunged to a new depth. R.H. had proven himself to be completely heartless.

The cab lost the last of its warmth, and a circle of breath frosted on the inside of the windshield. Jack shook himself free of his thoughts and jumped out of the truck. He'd better go back inside and find out how to contact Ingram's daughters about the Corvette. If he didn't, R.H. would do it himself. At least Jack could try to handle the situation tactfully.

The walk to the door seemed longer than before. An uncanny silence had settled over the wooded area behind the building, as heavy as the darkness that enveloped them. As he walked, Jack couldn't stop staring in that direction, peering between the heavy branches. They seemed menacing, as though they hid a dark and deadly secret. Had the murderer concealed himself there, watching Tom Ingram through the now-shuttered windows? Might he be there even now? The skin on Jack's arms crawled beneath a menacing stare that might, or might not, be imaginary. He rubbed his hands on his arms and quickened his pace toward the door.

TWO

Susanna watched from beneath the shield of her hand as Jack left the room. She was thankful he'd been with her when she had arrived here. What if she'd been alone when she found—she gulped—the body? Even so, she was glad to see Jack go. His presence was a painful reminder of that terrible time four years ago, and she couldn't bear to think about that right now. One tragedy at a time was all she could handle.

She glanced at the door to her boss's office, but thankfully she only saw the moving figures of police officers inside. More reminders. A terrible weight pressed on her chest as the reality of the situation struck her afresh.

Mr. Ingram was dead.

"Kathy, I don't know how much longer I'm going to be here," she whispered into the phone, aware of the silence that pervaded the outer office and the police officer who hovered near the doorway. "I'm sorry to dump her on you like this."

"I keep telling you, don't worry about it. Lizzie and Maddie have been playing ever since I picked them up from the babysitter. And I've already told them they might get to have a sleepover tonight. They were thrilled."

An ache throbbed behind Susanna's eyes. She closed

them and pressed her temples as hard as she could. "Thank you. I'll return the favor sometime."

The sound of shoes scuffing on the carpet in front of her drew Susanna's attention. She opened her eyes to find the detective who'd been questioning Jack for the past ten minutes standing in front of her. Plainclothes, but she'd be able to pinpoint him as a cop in a second if she met him on the street. He had the same arrogant air about him as the one she'd spoken with four years ago in Tennessee.

Stop it! This guy's probably on the up-and-up. Not all police officers are on some rich man's payroll.

She straightened and spoke into the phone. "I need to go. I'll call you when I know more."

When she had lowered the phone and started to stand, Detective Rollins stopped her with a gesture. "You can stay seated if you like. In fact, I'll join you."

He dropped into the chair beside her. Susanna placed her cell phone on the small table between them, next to an array of magazines she kept there for visitors to read while they waited for their appointments with Mr. Ingram. The hovering officer, a young man with a fresh face, approached to stand beside Rollins, his pen poised over a metal clipboard to record her words.

"I know this has been a shock, Ms. Trent." Rollins's smile held a world full of sympathy. "We've already taken Mr. Townsend's statement, but if you don't mind, I'd like for you to tell me everything that happened today."

Susanna drew a breath. "Mr. Ingram sent me to an auction out of town to buy a car for him. I didn't even come in to the office this morning because he wanted me to be there all day, to be sure I didn't miss the Corvette."

"Do you normally perform tasks like this for your boss?"

She hesitated. "Well, I'm his personal secretary, so I do

run errands for him often. Mr. Ingram is a widower and a busy executive, so if he needs someone to pick up his dry cleaning or prepare snacks for his poker club, I don't mind doing that. But this is the first time he's ever asked me to buy a car for him."

"Mr. Townsend told us that his father sent him there on the same errand. Is there something special about this Corvette?"

"Other than the fact that it's a really hot sports car? I don't think so." Susanna leaned forward to grab the handbag she had shoved beneath the chair. She fished inside until she found the auction catalog Mr. Ingram had given her yesterday. It was already opened to the appropriate page. "I wondered at the time if it was…" She bit her lip and battled feelings of disloyalty before she continued. "A midlife crisis."

Detective Rollins inspected the picture of the bright red Corvette—*bloodred* was the term Mr. Ingram had used to describe it. The uniformed officer peered over the detective's shoulder.

Rollins's lips twitched. "Speaking as a man of around the same age, I can affirm that if I could afford to buy a car to help me over a midlife crisis, that's one I'd pick." He returned the catalog, and Susanna shoved it back into the depths of her purse. "Ms. Trent, are you aware of anyone who might want to harm the victim?"

Since the moment she'd realized Mr. Ingram was dead, Susanna had been racking her brain trying to think who would do something so horrible to such a nice man. She'd drawn a complete blank.

"I can't think of anyone who would want to hurt Mr. Ingram. He is—" she bit her lip "—*was* well respected by everyone—all the employees here at Ingram Industries. The customers. Everyone."

"What about competitors?" Rollins tapped the issue of *American Coal* magazine that topped the stack on the table between them. "I imagine the coal industry is fairly competitive."

"Of course there's competition in any business, but nothing serious enough to kill someone over."

"A disgruntled employee, maybe? Anyone been fired lately?"

Susanna shook her head. "No."

Footsteps sounded in the hallway, and she looked up in time to see Jack step into the room. What was he doing here? She'd thought he had gone home.

After a quick glance in his direction, Rollins focused all his attention on her. "Who would be the most knowledgeable about the victim's day-to-day business dealings?"

Jack wandered over to her desk and picked up the framed photo on the corner, the one of her and Lizzie taken at last summer's company picnic.

"That would be me." She smoothed a lock of hair behind her ear. "I maintain Mr. Ingram's calendar, both business and personal. I arrange all his meetings, screen all his calls, draft his correspondence. And I can't think of a single issue that's come up lately with even the slightest bit of conflict."

The detective studied her for a moment, then gave a nod and slapped his hands on his knees before standing. "We'll need some information from you. The names of anyone who's had contact with the victim in the past few weeks, to begin with. His appointment calendar, phone records, things like that. Then we'll need the company's employee roster with contact information."

Susanna followed the detective's example and rose. A list began to compile itself in her mind, beginning with those who had closest contact with Mr. Ingram—the executives at Ingram Industries. And what about the board of directors? Detective Rollins would probably want their phone numbers, as well. Her conscience prickled, but she dismissed the feeling. No one would fault her for providing their private contact numbers to the police if it helped to apprehend a murderer.

"Hopefully it won't take you too long to pull that together. When you've finished, you're free to go." Rollins shifted his gaze to Jack. "Perhaps Mr. Townsend would be kind enough to escort you home."

A hot flush threatened to flood her cheeks. A glance at Jack's face showed he was as surprised at the detective's suggestion as her.

"Thank you, but that won't be necessary," she assured Rollins. "My car is in the parking lot."

The detective stopped in the act of walking away and turned to face her with a sober expression. "I don't want to frighten you, Ms. Trent, but I hope you understand how serious this situation is. You could be in danger yourself."

"Me?" Her voice came out in a frightened rush. "Why would I be in danger?"

Rollins's eyes flicked toward the inner office, where the low murmur of voices blended with the mechanical click of a camera. "A man has been killed in this office. Until we know more, we can't rule out the possibility that the killer's motive has something to do with the victim's business. And who is most closely acquainted with his business dealings?"

Susanna's mouth dried. Her lungs refused to cooperate, refused to draw in a breath. Fear paralyzed them.

The detective saw her reaction, and gave a nod. "Just so you understand the gravity of the situation. If you prefer, I'll have Officer Bledsoe make sure you get home safely."

Jack returned the picture to the desk and stepped

forward. "I don't mind following you home." The smile he flashed at her held a note of apology. "We need to talk about what happens with the car anyway."

Though she far preferred the officer as an escort, Susanna couldn't think of a polite reason to refuse Jack's offer. Her mind was still reeling from Detective Rollins's warning. And the image of Mr. Ingram's lifeless eyes. And the thought of going into her dark, empty house alone.

Mutely, Susanna nodded.

Light shone from the windows of the houses on either side of Susanna's, but hers was covered in blackness. Even the porch light was dark, burnt out a few weeks ago. She pulled her car into the driveway and made a mental note to replace the bulb as she slid out of the driver's seat. The rattle of Jack's diesel engine interrupted the neighborhood's peaceful silence. Susanna stood in the dim circle of light from her car's interior, her hand resting on the rim of the open door, as the pickup and trailer rolled to a stop at the curb in front of the house.

A sound broke the silence behind her. Startled, she whirled and peered into the deep shadow of overgrown evergreen shrubs that separated her house from the one next door. Was something there? Yes, the branches were moving. Her pulse kicked into high speed as she strained to make out details. Though clouds obscured the moon, there was no wind tonight. Was someone hiding there, between the houses?

The bushes moved again. In the second before she leaped back into her car, ready to slam the door and punch the lock button, she realized the movement was too low to be a person. She strained to discern black from pitch-black as the figure moved toward her. A tense breath left her lungs in a rush when the shadows materialized into the neighbor's cat, sauntering toward her with an unhurried gait. It disappeared beneath her car, apparently in search of a warm place to sleep. Susanna released her death grip on the door. How foolish of her, afraid of a cat. That detective had her jumping at shadows.

The truck's door slammed, and she turned to see Jack striding toward her across the grass.

Susanna closed her own car door and pointed toward the trailer as he approached. "I don't know what to do about the car. I don't have a garage to park it in."

Jack shoved his hands in the front pocket of his jeans, shoulders hunched against the cold. "I overheard you saying Ingram has two daughters. What about taking it to one of them?"

"The oldest lives in California, and the youngest is studying in Europe." She had given the police their contact information. Did they know yet that their father was dead? Susanna intended to call tomorrow, to see if they needed her to help with the arrangements.

"Does Ingram have a garage?"

Of course. Why didn't she think of that before they left the office? She massaged the back of her neck. Her brain wasn't working right tonight. Shock, probably. "Yes, he does. I guess we ought to go back to the office and get his house keys so we can take it over there."

Jack scuffed at the driveway with his shoe. "I hesitate to bring this up, but my father said he'd be happy to buy the Corvette now that Ingram—" he paused, embarrassed "—uh, won't be needing it. I'm sure he would store it at his house until the arrangements can be made."

For a moment, Susanna was speechless. How utterly mercenary of Jack's father to suggest such a thing while Mr. Ingram's strangled body still lay on the floor of his office. And how completely in character for a self-centered man who was used to getting whatever he wanted, regardless of the circumstances. People talked, and she'd heard rumors about R. H. Townsend and the ruthless way he ran his business. For office workers searching for a job, Townsend Steakhouses, Inc., was at the bottom of the list unless you were desperate.

She'd thought better of Jack, though. In the few hours she had known him, he'd seemed like a nice guy, with his generous offer to deliver the Corvette to Mr. Ingram. How could he bring himself to relay the request?

Or maybe she had misjudged Jack all along. His helpful gesture might not have been an act of kindness at all. Having failed to buy the car for his father at the auction, his good deed might have been a last-ditch effort to convince Mr. Ingram to sell it to him. Bitterly, Susanna realized she wasn't surprised. Her former fiancé, Bruce, would have acted the same heartless way if it meant getting something he wanted. Maybe Jack and Bruce were two of a kind. The thought soured her stomach. She was still searching for an appropriately scathing response when the porch light of the house across the street came on.

The front door opened and a figure appeared. Her neighbor, Kathy, made her way carefully across the street carrying a blanketed bundle.

"Hey, I saw you were here, so I thought I'd bring Lizzie home. She just fell asleep about half an hour ago."

Ignoring Jack, Susanna took the bundle from Kathy's arms. The child cocooned inside stirred during the transfer. A whimper sounded when the blanket fell open, exposing the little girl to the frigid night air.

"I don't wanna go home," Lizzie complained in a sleepy voice. "I wanna have a sleepover."

"Shh." Susanna tucked the blanket more snugly around

her. "We'll have a sleepover another time." She looked up at Kathy. "I can't thank you enough."

"No problem." She rubbed her hands on her arms and shivered. "I'll talk to you tomorrow, okay?" She flashed a quick smile at Jack as she left.

Jack watched, silent, as Susanna hugged the blanketed child close. She could see the questions in his wide eyes, but she left them unanswered. Her life was none of his business.

"I need to get her out of this cold air." She glanced toward the car trailer. "I hate to park an attention magnet like that Corvette openly in my driveway. Would it be all right if you left the trailer here tonight? Mr. Ingram's daughters will need to decide what they want to do with it." She pressed her lips together. "I'll get in touch with them tomorrow and pass along your offer."

He jerked away his curious stare at Lizzie, and whipped out a business card from his pocket. "Sure. Probably not a good idea to leave it on the street, so I'll put it in your driveway. My cell phone number is on that card. Just give me a call and let me know what they decide."

She took the card awkwardly while she balanced her sleeping bundle, and then turned her back on him to march toward the house.

"Here, let me get that." He leaped ahead of her up the concrete steps of her small porch and held his hand out for the keys. "I'll take a look inside, just to be on the safe side."

Susanna hesitated, but the thought of all those dark rooms inside—from now on she would leave a light burning, regardless of the electricity bill—made her decision for her. She handed him the keys and stood waiting while he unlocked the door, flipped the living-room light switch and stepped inside.

The warmth in the house was a comforting contrast to the biting cold of the porch. Susanna followed him in and stood, hugging Lizzie tight, while Jack made a tour through her small home. He was certainly thorough. By sound she tracked his progress through the kitchen, laundry, both bedrooms and the bathroom. He even peeked inside closets. Embarrassment that he was seeing the private rooms of her home warred with relief inside her, but she consciously grasped at the latter. The alarm created by Detective Rollins's warning was fading. She would feel much safer now, knowing a killer wasn't waiting to jump out at her the moment she and Lizzie were alone.

Jack reappeared in the living room. "Everything's fine. I made sure all the windows were locked, too."

"Thank you." She forced herself to smile. This guy was certainly an anomaly. One minute he offended her with an inappropriate offer to buy the Corvette, and the next he was going the extra mile to make sure she felt safe. "I appreciate that."

"No problem. Oh. Here." He extracted a key ring with a single key from his pocket and, since her hands were full, set it on the coffee table. "The key to the car trailer."

He left, and Susanna stood in the doorway watching as he crossed the yard and climbed into the pickup. The engine roared to life, and he maneuvered the trailer backward into her driveway. When it came to a stop on the other side of her car, she pushed the door closed and threw the dead bolt before heading down the short hallway to Lizzie's bedroom.

She was still getting the child settled in bed when the engine revved again. A peek through the pink curtains revealed the taillights disappearing down the street. When the truck turned the corner, a wave of anxiety threatened her composure.

What if the detective was right? What if someone is watching, waiting to get me alone? I should have asked Jack to check the backyard, too.

With an effort, she forced the haunting image of Mr. Ingram's body from her mind. If she dwelt on thoughts like that, she would become paranoid. She posed no threat to whoever killed Mr. Ingram, because she didn't know anything. She hadn't even been near the office at all today.

There's nothing to worry about. I need to relax and get some sleep. Things always look better in the morning.

Still, she decided to make one more round through the house and check all the locks before she got ready for bed. Just to be sure.

THREE

Jack steered the pickup through Susanna's modest neighborhood. Though he had lived in Lexington his whole life, he'd never been on these streets. The yards were all clean and neatly landscaped, as far as he could tell in the dark. Mature trees testified to the age of the homes, which were single-story rectangles made of brick. The small size of Susanna's had surprised him. The whole house would fit inside the kitchen in his family home, where he had grown up and where his father still lived. Even Jack's apartment was half again as big. But every room in Susanna's house had been spotlessly clean, the decorations tastefully elegant. The little girl's room had pink frills everywhere, an overflowing toy box and a bedspread with princesses.

And what about that child? He didn't glimpse much more than a quick peek of a smooth cheek and bow-shaped lips inside the blanket. The picture on the desk at Ingram Industries had shown a happy little girl with sparkling blue eyes and blond hair, the same bright shade as Susanna's. The child was around two or three years old, if he was to take a guess. Susanna obviously wasn't married, since she and the girl lived alone. Divorced maybe? Or maybe she had never married. Was the child's father in the picture at all? He gauged Susanna's age at mid-twenties, plenty old enough to have a three-year-old daughter. Although, now that he thought about it, that was pretty young to have attained the status of executive secretary for a coal magnate like Ingram. How had she managed to land such an important job?

Jack gave a soundless laugh as he exited the neighborhood with a right turn onto the main road. What was this preoccupation with a woman and her child? They were none of his business. He'd done what he could for them, made sure the house was empty and secure. Though personally he thought Detective Rollins's warning a bit on the dramatic side. The police had no idea why Ingram had been killed. To assume his secretary was in danger was too big a leap to make sense, in Jack's opinion. But the police had to be extracautious, he supposed.

Lord, keep her safe tonight, please. And help her to get some rest. She's had a pretty awful day.

The quick prayer on Susanna's behalf put that part of his mind to rest. He had done the only thing—the *best* thing—he could do for her.

The traffic light up ahead turned yellow, and Jack slowed to a stop as it changed to red, gingerly pumping the brakes in case the evening's sleet had left icy patches. A right turn would take him to the affluent neighborhood where he had grown up. He hadn't lived there since college and his first apartment off campus, where he'd encountered a peaceful existence he hadn't dreamed possible in the years of living under R.H.'s critical eye. Cheri, his older sister, had escaped four years before him when she went to Cornell University. She had never returned to Kentucky. Jack visited her in New York as often as he could.

A couple of cars passed by in front of him heading in the direction of his family home, where R.H. no doubt was still hard at work in his office, though the clock on Jack's dash read ten-fourteen. Their earlier phone call replayed itself in his mind, as conversations with R.H. were wont to do. There had been one moment when Jack thought he detected a trace of emotion in the astringent voice. When R.H. had learned of Ingram's death, he'd said, "That's terrible. Just terrible." He'd sounded shocked, and a little bit… vulnerable?

No, Jack must have imagined that part. Vulnerability was something he'd never seen his father display. It was a weakness, and R.H. had no patience for weakness in any form. He'd excised it from his life many years ago, when Mom died. But it was natural to feel shock at the violent death of a friend. Ingram and R.H. shared a lot in common, after all. They were roughly the same age. Ran in the same social circles. They both headed up powerful corporations, though in different industries. R.H. must have identified with Ingram to some extent. The death had to come as a blow, perhaps even give him a glimpse of his own mortality.

The light changed from red to green. At the same moment Jack took his foot off the brake, he came to a decision. He turned on his blinker, checked the mirror and made a quick right turn. If R.H. was feeling Ingram's death personally, even a little, then he shouldn't be alone. His questions might turn toward spiritual matters, and if they did, Jack wanted to be there with the answers he had found himself. No doubt he would be slapped down yet again, but the man *was* his father. Beneath the ridicule and the harsh behavior, Jack knew R.H. loved him and Cheri as much as he could. As much as he was able.

He punched in the code to open the gate at the entrance to the exclusive neighborhood, and then steered the truck through the familiar streets. The homes here were a far different style than the ones he had just seen. The price tag for many of them ranged into seven-digit territory, and every lawn had the unmistakable look of hours of care by professional landscapers.

Three turns and Jack arrived at the cul-de-sac where he had grown up. He pulled into the driveway of the house and followed the graceful, rosebush-lined curve around to the back. But the windows he'd expected to see lit up, the ones to his father's study, were dark. In fact, there were no lights on anywhere in the house. Jack checked the clock on the dashboard again. Not even ten-thirty, and R.H. was already in bed?

A niggling worry started in his mind, like an itch he couldn't ignore. R.H. never went to bed before midnight. Was he sick? Had Ingram's death affected him more than he let on?

Jack parked the truck and hopped out. He went to the back door, but hesitated before he put his key in the lock. It was possible his father had simply gone to bed earlier than usual. Even if he were upset by Ingram's death, he wouldn't appreciate Jack's interference. In fact, any concern Jack was bold enough to voice would no doubt be met with scorn, and probably another angry tirade.

The window in the back door was covered with custom-fitted blinds, and Jack could see nothing through it. After a moment of indecision, he turned toward his truck. Tomorrow at the office he'd mention that he stopped by to give him an update on the Corvette, but left when he realized R.H. had turned in early. Maybe he'd learn something from the reaction he received.

He followed the cobbled walkway toward his pickup and passed the garage window. The blinds stood open and he glanced inside. He skidded to a stop. It was probably just the darkness, but from this distance it looked as if the garage bay nearest the window was empty. Curious, he stepped over the knee-high shrubs to take a closer look. His shoes scuffed in the winter mulch of the flower bed as he approached the window.

The three-car garage normally housed two vehicles. One bay had remained empty for as long as Jack could remember. R.H.'s main car was a BMW, and that was parked in its regular place, the bay closest to the door leading into the house. But he also had another car, a Lexus SUV, which he used on the rare occasions when he drove out in the country to the hunting lodge, or when the city roads were icy. The SUV was missing.

R.H. was not at home.

When Jack called earlier he had dialed the house phone, so he knew his father had been at home ninety minutes ago. Where would he go this late at night?

Though weariness dragged at Susanna's body, sleep refused to come. The novel on her bedside table failed to either hold her attention or coax her to sleep. She gave up on the book, turned off the light and closed her eyes. But all she could see was the image of the body sprawled on the floor. Her eyes flew open. Maybe a hot cup of herbal tea would help her relax. Resigned, she got out of bed, slid her feet into her slippers and went to the kitchen.

A few minutes later, she carried a steaming mug to the soft comfort of the living-room sofa. Her purse lay on the cushion where she'd tossed it, the packet of papers she'd received from the auction inside. The last errand she would ever perform for her boss. She dropped onto the couch and sipped from her tea. There had been something else in the plastic envelope with the papers and keys, but she'd been too busy trying to find a company to transport the car tonight to pay much attention to it. And since then, she'd been…well, occupied.

She set the mug on the table, fished out the envelope and upended it onto the cushion beside her. Out tumbled the owner's manual, registration, car title signed by the previous owner and a set of keys on a metal ring along with a key tag bearing the Corvette emblem. The bulk of the contents was a thick stack of papers held together with a large rubber band documenting the car's maintenance history, which was apparently important to the value of a classic automobile. The auctioneer had made a big deal out of mentioning it.

Susanna fanned through the papers. They were in date order going all the way back to 1980, the year the car was manufactured. Oil changes, brake pad replacements, a receipt for new tires. Something dropped out of the bundle and landed on the cushion beside the owner's manual—a small canvas pouch with a drawstring opening cinched shut. Curious, she opened it and emptied the contents into the palm of her hand: a silver coin, about the size and weight of a half dollar. One side was embossed with a single word—*nine*. She flipped it over. The other side contained the digit—*9*.

A comment from the car's previous owner, whom she had met briefly while sitting at the auction desk signing papers, came back to her. He'd smiled as he shook her hand and said, "Congratulations. You got number nine." She had assumed the man was a dealer or something, and the Corvette was the ninth car he'd sold today.

She weighed the token in the palm of her hand. How odd. Why would he put numbered coins in with each of the cars he sold? Maybe it had something to do with Corvettes, like a numbered painting or something. Or maybe it had something to do with the auction. Sort of like a proof of purchase, perhaps? She held the token up to the light and inspected it carefully for any other markings. Nothing. No

Corvette emblems, nor the auction house's logo. She'd have to remember to ask Mr. Ingram about—

Reality slapped at her, cutting off the thought unfinished. She'd never be able to ask Mr. Ingram anything, ever again.

In a flash, the events of the day caught up with her. She replaced the coin in its pouch, stuffed everything back into the envelope and shoved it inside her purse. Then she switched off the lamp, clutched a throw pillow to her chest and tucked her feet beneath her. Tears held too long in check burned her eyes and blurred her vision. She could hardly believe Mr. Ingram was gone. Memories paraded through her mind, each one bringing a fresh rush of tears, until her cheeks were raw from salty rivers flowing over them. After an eternity they slowed and finally stopped. Numbness gradually stole over her, and Susanna slept.

A clang jarred her awake. She jerked upright. What was that noise? Had it come from inside the house?

The digital clock on the DVD player read nearly two-thirty. Heart thudding heavily inside her chest, Susanna rose as quietly as she could from the couch. She tiptoed across the carpet to the front door and checked the lock. Still securely closed. She hurried down the hallway and into Lizzie's room. Maybe the child had fallen out of bed again. The weight in her chest lightened a fraction at the sight of the little girl sleeping peacefully in her bed, tousled blond curls splayed across her pillow. She was safe.

And yet, if the sound hadn't originated from Lizzie, where had it come from? Quickly Susanna went through the house, checking every room, every lock on the windows. All was as it should be. Had she dreamed it, maybe? No, she didn't think so. She could hear an echo of it still, pulling her from sleep with a metallic clank.

The noise must have come from outside.

Mr. Ingram's Corvette! She hurried back to the front room and, standing in the dark, parted the front curtain a fraction, just the width of her eye. The sky had cleared and white moonlight illuminated the yard. She saw no movement at all. On the other side of her Toyota, the trailer was in the exact place Jack had left it.

She let the curtains fall back into place. Maybe she *had* imagined the noise. Or maybe it had come from a passing vehicle. Or she dreamed it.

Her tea mug sat on the end table, half full of cold tea. She picked it up and carried it to the kitchen. Dim, white light filtered through the miniblinds in the window above the sink. As she emptied the contents of the mug down the drain, she peeked into the dark backyard. All was still. Not even a breeze stirred the branches of the tall evergreen hedge that bordered her yard.

A noise close by sent alarm zipping down her spine. It was coming from the door. Breath caught in her throat, she crept toward it. Horror stole over her as she watched the door knob turn slowly. Just a tiny bit, a fraction of movement, back and forth, as someone on the other side jiggled the handle.

Susanna couldn't stop the scream that tore from her throat. She raced from the room, snatching her cell phone off the kitchen counter as she ran. By the time she got to Lizzie's bedroom and slammed the door, she had already punched 9-1-1.

FOUR

"I'd fallen asleep on the couch," Susanna told the policeman standing in her living room, "and a noise woke me up. I'm almost positive it came from the car trailer in the driveway."

The young man wasn't one of the officers she'd seen at Ingram Industries last night, nor his partner, who at the moment was investigating the backyard with a flashlight.

He nodded. "Have you checked the trailer?"

"Are you kidding?" Susanna clutched Lizzie, whose arms and legs were still wrapped tightly around her even though the child was starting to drift back to sleep. "We shoved the dresser in front of the bedroom door and hid in the closet until you got here."

"That was a smart move, ma'am."

She glanced toward the window. "I'm worried about the car, though. It's extremely expensive, and it doesn't belong to me."

"I'll check it out."

When he turned toward the door, she stopped him. "Here. You'll need this."

She scooped up the trailer key, which was still where Jack had left it on the coffee table. As he left the house, she considered putting Lizzie back to bed so she could check on the Corvette. But the child had been terrified to be awakened by Susanna's panicked shrieks, and she didn't want to risk her waking up alone while everyone else was outside. Instead, she scooped up a throw blanket from the armchair, bundled it around the little girl and followed the officer outside. Bitterly cold air slapped at Susanna's face as she hurried down the porch steps and across the short walkway to where the officer stood at the rear of the trailer.

"The lock appears to be intact." The man pulled on a thin rubber glove and, with a finger and thumb, carefully tested the handle.

To her surprise, the lever pushed all the way down.

The officer's eyebrows rose. "Are you sure you locked it?"

She thought back, picturing the scene in the auction house's rear parking lot. Jack had locked the door after they'd loaded the car inside, hadn't he? She couldn't remember. "Well, no, I'm not positive. But I'm pretty sure we did."

The officer pulled on the handle, and the door swung open. Breath caught in her chest, she peered inside.

The sight of the red sports car sent a wave of relief flooding through her tense muscles. "It's still there." Maybe Jack had simply forgotten to lock the door.

The policeman climbed into the trailer and unclipped a small flashlight from his belt. The Corvette's body gleamed in the powerful beam.

He gave a low, admiring whistle. "This is a beautiful car."

"Is it all right?" Susanna asked.

The beam flashed around. "Not a scratch on her." He dropped down on his haunches and peered beneath. "The straps are still in place, too. I don't think anyone's messed with this car."

"Thank goodness."

The officer circled to the passenger side, still examining the unblemished paint. Susanna turned toward the house. Now that she'd satisfied herself the Corvette was safe, she could go back inside where it was warm. Obviously the noise that had woken her earlier hadn't come from the trailer. She took a step as the officer opened the passenger door and aimed his flashlight inside. Out of the corner of her eye, she saw him pull the seat upright and heard a distant *snap* as it clicked into place.

Her foot halted. Was the passenger seat pushed forward when they put the car in the trailer?

No. It wasn't. She was positive about that.

She returned to stand at the rear of the trailer. "I think someone's been in there."

The officer's head emerged from his examination of the interior. "What makes you think so?"

"I'm sure that seat wasn't pushed forward. And why would Jack make a point of giving me the key if he was going to leave the trailer unlocked?" Her arms tightened around Lizzie. Detective Rollins's warning left an ominous echo in her mind. "What if the person who killed Mr. Ingram came after his car?"

A noise behind her made her whirl, but it was only the second officer coming from the backyard.

"Nothing back there, ma'am. No signs at all of an intruder." His gaze rose from her face to his partner's inside the trailer.

Did she imagine it, or did a secretive look pass between them? She could almost hear the older officer's thoughts. *Woman without a man around for protection. Panics over nothing.* Despite the frigid air, heat flared up her neck. "I know I heard a noise outside, and I know someone jiggled the knob on my back door."

Before the silence became uncomfortable, the officer in the trailer hopped down to the ground. "I have a theory. I think it was teenagers."

His partner nodded, as though in agreement.

"Why do you say that?" Susanna asked. "Did you find something inside the car?"

He shook his head as he slid his flashlight back into place on his belt. "If it was a car thief, they would have been more prepared. They would have come with a truck and hauled off the trailer with the car inside. We've had trouble with teenagers prowling around town late at night. Some gang activity. Instances of vandalism. My guess is the trailer caught their attention. Since there's no sign that the lock was forced, we have to assume the door wasn't locked to begin with."

Susanna would have argued that point, but without a call to Jack she couldn't say for certain. And there was no way she was calling Jack at three in the morning. At least the officer believed her that someone had been here.

He nodded toward the Corvette. "Taking a car like that out for a joyride would be almost irresistible. They probably searched the interior to see if they could find the keys."

"But then why try to break into my house?"

The other officer answered. "They probably figured someone who would leave a car like that in an unlocked trailer wouldn't be too careful with their house, either. They may have just been checking to see if they could get inside the house and get the keys. You scared them off when you screamed." His expression grew sober. "It's a good thing you locked your doors. If they were on drugs, you never know what could have happened to you and your little girl."

Susanna turned to look into the deep shadows of the backyard. The scenario did seem feasible, assuming Jack had simply forgotten to lock the trailer. She certainly intended to ask him about that the next time she spoke with him.

Still, having someone try to break into her house the same night Mr. Ingram was killed seemed like an awfully big coincidence. What would that detective think? She almost hated to bring up the man's name, because he reminded her so much of the detective she'd spoken with during that awful business back in Tennessee. "I don't know. Maybe we should contact Detective Rollins."

"Oh, don't worry, ma'am." The first officer closed the trailer door. "We'll give him a full report."

He turned the key in the lock, tested the handle to be sure it was secure, and handed her the key ring.

She held Lizzie in place with one hand and took the key with the other. "So you think we'll be safe the rest of the night?"

"Yes, ma'am, I do." The officer glanced at his watch, then smiled at Lizzie's sleeping form. "You should take a cue from your daughter and try to get a few hours' sleep. We'll make some extra patrols up and down this street for the rest of the night, keep an eye on things. Just to be on the safe side."

The two officers headed for their cruisers. Susanna watched them for a moment, until an icy breeze blew against her back. Lizzie should be inside, where it was warm. She hurried up the walkway, climbed the steps and let herself into the house.

Sleep, the officer had said. After all she'd been through? Right. The two hours she'd managed to doze on the couch earlier would have to last her a while. No way she'd be able to sleep any more tonight.

When she'd deposited Lizzie in bed—Susanna's, not the little girl's—she returned to the front of the house. A peek through the curtains revealed one of the cruisers still parked at the curb. The sight eased the mounting tension a fraction. A light illuminated the younger officer, his head bent over something on the seat beside him. Typing his report on a computer, probably. Good. Hopefully he'd have a lot to say, and it would take a long time. If the teenagers returned, the presence of a police officer would be a strong deterrent.

But the cruiser would leave eventually. She tried to ignore the panicky feeling that made her breath shallow. She was not normally the hysterical type, but the events of the past several hours would make anyone paranoid. If only she had a weapon of some sort. Not a gun, because she wouldn't know how to use one if she had it. But a baseball bat, maybe, or a crowbar. A glance around the room revealed no likely weapons. She went into the kitchen, opened the knife drawer and examined the dangerous blade of the butcher knife.

No. Someone would have to get far too close for a knife to do any good. Besides, she was a weakling. If anyone got into the house, she and Lizzie were done for. Her best defense was to make sure nobody got in to begin with.

She slid out one of the sturdy wooden chairs from the dinette set that had belonged to her mother, tilted it on its back two legs and wedged the backrest under the door handle. There. They'd have to chop through the door with an ax to get past that. She'd use another chair on the front door and a third for her bedroom door. She and Lizzie would be safe inside.

Before she left the room, she returned to the drawer and grabbed the butcher knife, too. Just in case.

* * *

Susanna awoke Friday morning to Lizzie's happy chatter.

"I slept with you, Susu!" The child hopped like an excited frog on the mattress. "We had a sleepover."

Morning sunlight filtered through the yellow bedroom curtains and filled the room with a cheery glow. Susanna stretched and glanced at the clock. Eight twenty-seven. In all the chaos of last night she had forgotten to set the alarm, and now they'd overslept. She couldn't remember the last time she'd slept until eight-thirty on a weekday. Of course, she hadn't expected to sleep at all, and couldn't remember dropping off. Exhaustion must have finally caught up with her.

Lizzie bounced once more before settling on the mattress beside her. "Is it Cartoon Day?"

At three years old, Lizzie had yet to learn the days of the week. She knew she went to her babysitter's house on workdays, and on Saturday she was allowed to spend a couple of hours in front of the television watching her favorite cartoons.

Susanna shook her head. "No, sweetie, it's not Saturday. It's Friday, a workday."

Although, after what she'd been through, nobody would blame her for taking a day off. They could lounge around the house in their pajamas and watch one of Lizzie's favorite Disney DVDs. Filling her mind with images of princesses in beautiful dresses sounded far more appealing than the somber faces she would encounter at Ingram Industries today.

Guilt immediately flared. The employees would be shocked when they showed up for work to discover Mr. Ingram had been killed. Everyone loved him, and they'd all be saddened by his loss. They'd be worried, too, about the status of the company and their jobs. Plus, the board members would need to make some decisions. No doubt there would be an emergency meeting to organize. As Mr. Ingram's executive secretary, she needed to be at work today.

With a resolute hand, she peeled back the blanket and slid out of bed. Lizzie bounded after her, then caught sight of the chair wedged against the door. The room filled with childish giggles as she pointed.

"Susu, you brought a chair to bed with you."

"Silly me, huh?"

In the light of day, her paranoia of the night before did seem a little absurd. But only for a moment, until she remembered the horror of that rattling doorknob and the unlocked car trailer.

Before falling asleep, she'd come to a decision about the Corvette. It couldn't stay here. She wanted no part of the kind of attention a car like that attracted. Selling it to Jack's father without talking to Mr. Ingram's daughters was out of the question, but it had to go to storage or something until they could decide what to do with it. That was at the top of her To Do list this morning.

On her bedside table lay her cell phone, the key to the trailer and Jack's business card. He expected her to call when she knew whether or not Mr. Ingram's daughters were willing to sell the Corvette. Would he mind transporting it to a storage facility instead?

Probably not. Regardless of his father's reputation, he seemed like a nice guy. Certainly friendlier and more helpful than… She steeled her thoughts away from the direction they wanted to take. The little girl jumping with glee on the mattress provided a constant reminder that she couldn't be too careful when it came to rich bachelors like Jack Townsend.

Still, she had no choice. Much as she hated to do it, she needed to ask him for a favor.

Resigned, she reached for her phone.

FIVE

"I really think that trailer was locked when I left here last night." Jack stood in Susanna's driveway, at the rear of the car trailer. Her call had interrupted a slow morning at work, so he'd jumped at the chance to leave.

He placed a gloved hand on the chrome handle and jerked downward, but the lock held fast. "I remember doing it after I secured the car inside."

Susanna looked every inch the cool executive secretary this morning. He had no trouble picturing her side-by-side in a conference room with Alice, his father's long-suffering assistant, though Susanna's dark blue suit somehow accented her feminine shape in a way Alice's clothing never had. Yesterday at the auction Susanna's hair had swung free, but this morning she'd smoothed it back from her head and captured it in some sort of twist that made her look both elegant and professional. Not a hint of the vulnerability he'd glimpsed last night was in evidence in her cool demeanor. In fact, Jack found this version of Susanna a little intimidating.

She folded her arms. "Maybe the teenagers picked the lock."

Jack inspected the lever. No damage, and no telltale gouges in the metal. "It hasn't been broken or anything.

You wouldn't think teenagers would be expert enough to pick a lock without damaging it."

He looked up in time to see her eyes go a tiny bit rounder as she raised them to his. "You don't think it was teenagers?"

Was that a note of fear in her voice? Well, Jack could hardly blame her if it was. She'd seen a gruesome sight last night, and then been scared half out of her wits by someone trying to get into her house. Even hysteria would be understandable.

Doubt about the police officer's explanation plagued him. If the events she'd described were related to Ingram's murder, she was right to be afraid. On the other hand, teenagers were notoriously curious, and the appearance of a car trailer in a driveway where one had never been was certain to attract their attention.

"I don't know," he admitted. "And who knows? Maybe I didn't turn the key all the way when I locked it. I *think* I did, but it's one of those automatic things you do and then can't remember." Jack was ninety-five percent positive he'd locked the trailer, but that left five percent of uncertainty. "Regardless, I think you're right to store the Corvette somewhere else. Where would you like me to take it?"

She cast a quick glance toward the house. "I found a place over on Winchester Road, but they didn't answer their phone when I called. I thought I'd follow you over there and make the arrangements."

"What if they don't have any inside spaces available? I don't think you want to park that car out in the open, exposed to the weather."

Her fingers tightened on her arms. "I didn't think of that. I just assumed they'd have room for it. I should have called someplace else, but I slept late, and then…" Even, white teeth appeared, clamped down on her lower lip, then disappeared as quickly. "Would you mind following me to the office? The weather's supposed to be good today. We can unload it in the parking lot, so you can take your trailer. I'm sure it'll be okay there for a few hours, and that will give me time to find a place to store it before dark. I'll get someone to help me drive it over after I've made the arrangements."

Jack hesitated. A thought had occurred to him, but he wasn't sure how she would receive the offer. "Listen, I'm not in any hurry to use the trailer. I typically haul motorcycles and camping gear in it in nice weather, so I won't need it for a few more months. We could leave the car in it until Ingram's daughters decide what they want to do."

"You mean store it at your house?"

"No, I live in a town house, and my garage is full." He couldn't meet her eyes as he made the suggestion. "But my father lives in a gated community, and the end of his driveway is behind the house, not visible from the road. I'm sure he wouldn't mind if we park the trailer there for a few days."

He risked a glance at her face, and encountered icy eyes narrowed to mere slits. "Your father."

All right, yes. The suggestion might look suspicious, given R.H.'s inappropriate offer to buy the car last night. Jack opened his mouth to suggest that they call the storage place again, but stopped when she placed a hand on his arm.

"Thank you. That's a nice gesture, and I appreciate it." Her smile looked a little forced, but at least it appeared. "I'm sure the car will be safe there, and it'll be a relief not to have to worry about it anymore." Her shoulders heaved with a slight laugh. "I've got far too many other things to do today."

The front door of the house opened and a girl with

golden curls appeared. Ah, the sleeping child from last night, and from the picture on Susanna's desk. She didn't step out of the house, but shouted toward them in a high pitched voice, "Can I watch *Beauty and the Beast?*"

Susanna shook her head. "No, honey. I've got to go to work. But why don't you put the DVD in your backpack? Maybe Miss Christy will let you watch it after lunch." Her voice held a softer tone than he had yet heard.

"Okay." The little girl disappeared, and the door slammed shut.

When Susanna turned back to him, her expression was once again all business. "So, I'll call you as soon as Mr. Ingram's daughters let me know something about the car. In the meantime, please thank your father for being so helpful."

Was there a hint of disdain in her eyes as she uttered the last word? Jack couldn't be sure, but he wouldn't be surprised. The attitude was understandable, too. R.H. was well-known in this town, no doubt by reputation as much as by name.

"You have my number," he answered. "Let me know if there's anything else I can do to help."

"Thank you."

A touch of ice may have melted from her gaze, or it might merely have been a trick of the sunlight. In the next moment, she turned toward the house. Interesting woman. And not hard on the eyes, either. Jack watched until the front door closed behind her, then set to work hooking up the car trailer to his truck.

The headquarters of Townsend Steakhouses, Inc., were located in a glass-encased building on the southeast side of Lexington. After Jack dropped off the Corvette and trailer at his father's house, he headed there. Not that his schedule held any pressing appointments requiring his presence today. Or any day, if the truth were told. His absence would probably pass without notice. Though the sign on his office door proclaimed him to be the Vice President of Supply, he held the title in name only. Every decision related to their suppliers was made exclusively by the company's CEO, and everyone knew it.

He stepped off the elevator on the third floor, where the executive offices lined the windows overlooking an ice-covered pond with a fountain that, during the summer, sprayed blue-green water into the air. Instead of turning right toward his office he strode down the carpeted hallway to his left, toward the extralarge corner office from where his father dominated an important segment of the casual dining industry.

Alice Lester sat behind an immaculate desk, her fingers alive with near-silent activity as they danced over a keyboard. In the world of administrative assistants, Alice was considered among the best. Jack knew of multiple job offers she'd received from executives who had hoped to lure her away with high salaries and exclusive perks, but to everyone's amazement she had refused them all. She bore the brunt of R.H.'s temper with an unruffled manner that was nothing short of amazing. Jack had no idea how much his father was paying Alice, but it must have been a lot. Why else would she put up with him for over fifteen years?

Jack couldn't help comparing her to the other executive secretary he'd just left. Instead of Susanna's blond twist, Alice hacked off her thick dark hair, which was veined liberally with steely gray, just below her ears. Her charcoal suit was no less stylish than Susanna's, but it hung shapelessly from rounded shoulders that hunched slightly forward. Only a faint peachy blush on her lips betrayed any evidence of makeup.

And yet, Alice was one of the things that made the atmosphere on the executive floor of this building tolerable. Her unflappable composure played a consistent and dramatic counterpoint to R.H.'s hot temper.

She pulled her gaze away from the computer monitor at his approach. Concerned creases instantly appeared in her brow. "Jack, your father told me about Tom Ingram's death. I'm so sorry you had to see that. It must have been terrible."

Jack refused to allow the scene from last night to replay in his mind. "It was pretty awful. Even worse for his secretary, though."

She shivered. "The poor girl. I can't imagine."

Jack nodded toward the closed office door behind her. "Is R.H. available? I need to talk to him a minute."

"Richard is in there with him, but I don't think they're doing anything that can't be interrupted."

Richard Stratton was his father's chief of staff, his henchman on virtually any project related to personnel. Everyone in the company had expected R.H. to appoint Jack to that role last year, when the previous chief of staff resigned to take a job with a competitor. The announcement that R.H. had hired an outsider over his son had been an obvious slight, and more embarrassing than Jack would have thought possible. Still, Richard seemed competent enough, and Jack didn't hold his position against him.

"I'll just be a minute," Jack promised as he headed for the office. He rapped on the door twice, then pushed it open.

R.H. was seated behind his desk, a drawerless oval that would have been impressive if the thick glass top were kept clear. Instead, only the center was empty. Stacks of paper lined the outside edge, not messy but certainly not neat. Taller piles littered the carpet around the desk, and even one of the guest chairs contained a stack of past issues of *Restaurant Magazine*.

Richard stood beside R.H.'s chair, leaning forward to read from a sheet of paper in his boss's hand. When Jack stepped into the room, he straightened with a faint smile of greeting.

R.H. slammed down the paper. "There you are. I looked for you earlier, but your office was dark." He made a show of studying his watch. "How much am I paying you to work half days?"

Jack forced his facial muscles to remain relaxed. "I was here at seven this morning, but I had to run an errand. That's what I wanted to talk to you about."

Richard stepped out from behind the desk. "I'll leave you two alone."

"That's not necessary," Jack told him.

"It's all right. I've got some things to do." He paused as he passed Jack in the doorway, and looked back at R.H. "I'll get back with you on that by lunchtime."

R.H. dismissed him with a wave, then began straightening the stack of papers in front of him.

Jack stepped up to the front edge of the desk. "I got a call from Tom Ingram's secretary this morning. Someone tried to break into the trailer in her driveway last night. She wanted to move the Corvette into storage, but I told her it would be safe at the house for a few days. I just ran over there and dropped it off."

R.H. paused in the act of tapping the edge of the papers on the desk. "The Corvette is at my house?"

"That's right." Jack figured his father would be pleased at the news. And who knew? Maybe possession of the car would prove to his advantage. Ingram's daughters might be more willing to sell it to him if they didn't have to bother with getting it out of storage and transporting it to him. "I haven't heard whether or not his daughters want to sell it, though I'm sure they'll let us know within a couple days."

His father cleared a place on the edge of his desk for the now-neat stack of papers. "I don't think I'm interested anymore."

It took a moment for the words to sink in. "You don't want the Corvette?"

R.H. glared upward. "I didn't stutter, did I?"

Jack returned the stare, speechless. R.H.'s behavior regarding this Corvette had been bizarre from the very beginning. He'd never shown any interest in classic cars until a week ago. Then he sent Jack to buy the car sight unseen. Last night he'd been so eager to get his hands on it he'd practically rejoiced over Ingram's death. But now, when the car was parked in his driveway, he no longer wanted it.

And just where had he gone at ten-thirty last night?

Jack cast around for a way to ask his question casually, but couldn't come up with one. Finally, he blurted out, "I came by the house late last night. You weren't there."

For the span of a breath, R.H.'s face froze. An expression Jack had never seen flashed onto his features, and then was gone before it could be identified.

"Why were you there?" The question flew at Jack like an accusation.

"I thought you might appreciate someone to talk to about your friend's death."

A harsh laugh blasted through his lips. "I don't need to talk to anybody."

Jack pressed the point. "Then where did you go?"

"I was hungry. Went out to grab a hamburger." The

explanation came quickly, followed immediately by the return of his habitual glare. "What business is it of yours what I do with my time?"

Jack held up his palms. "None at all. I was just concerned."

R.H.'s hands slapped down on the desk. "You have enough to *concern* yourself without poking your nose into my business. You do have a job here, you know. Try focusing on it for a while instead of wasting your time playing the hero for some pretty little secretary."

An angry heat flooded Jack's face. He executed his job—what few responsibilities he managed to pry from his father's tight-fisted grip—with precision and competence. To imply that he didn't was insulting.

Patience, Lord. Give me patience.

Not a single appropriate response to such a ridiculous accusation came to mind. As Jack had learned to do at young age, he opted for a silent exit over angry words that would only lead to more conflict. He turned his back on his father and headed for the door.

R.H.'s voice stopped him. "One more thing. You have your own place. If one of your friends wants to store something, you take it. Don't offer my house as a storage facility."

Jack's jaw clenched. He didn't let out the breath trapped in his lungs until he'd gotten to his own office and closed the door behind him.

SIX

A cluster of whispering accounting clerks near the coffee-pot fell silent when Susanna rounded the corner and headed for her office. After a moment's pause, they moved toward her as a group and intersected her before she reached her doorway. She welcomed the distraction. Walking through the metal door she'd used last night had proven more difficult than she anticipated, and had required a few moments to gather her nerve before she could touch the handle.

One of the younger clerks grabbed her coat sleeve. "It's so horrible. I can hardly believe it."

She covered the girl's hand with her own and pressed. "I know."

"Is it true what they're saying?" A second wide-eyed girl's voice dropped to a whisper. "That *you* found the body?"

Susanna's throat clenched shut at the memory. She managed a nod.

The girl sucked in a noisy breath. "Oh, I'm so sorry."

One of the office doors on the other side of the large room opened and the accounting manager emerged, followed by a uniformed police officer. The group quickly dispersed, each clerk hurrying away to disappear in the sea of cubicles in the open room. Josie, the manager, caught sight of Susanna and made her way around the corner of shoulder-high divider walls, the officer in tow.

Susanna stepped through her office doorway, took off her gloves and shrugged out of her coat. When she'd hung it on a hook, the pair entered.

Red blotches marred the skin beneath Josie's eyes and around her nose. Fresh tears glittered behind the small lenses of her glasses. She grabbed for Susanna's hand. "Such a tragedy."

Susanna squeezed the woman's fingers, her glance sliding to the officer. His face was vaguely familiar. One of the crew who had been here last night, no doubt.

"Is Detective Rollins here?" She might not entirely trust the man, but she wanted to make sure he'd received the report about the middle-of-the-night incident at her house. And what was his opinion of the teenager theory?

The officer shook his head. "He was here this morning to speak with some of the employees, but he went back down to the station."

Josie lifted the glasses off her nose and wiped her eyes. "He talked to Dan and Steven."

The VPs in charge of operations and finance. Susanna nodded. They were the two most senior members of the executive staff, and the ones most qualified to make the necessary decisions to keep things running. The board would probably name one of them as the new CEO.

Tears blurred her own eyes. Impatient, she batted them away. There was too much work to do to give in to grief. Mr. Ingram would want her to maintain a clear head.

The officer held up his clipboard. "I'm taking statements from the employees, trying to see if there are any leads to follow up on. Probably be here most of the day."

Josie straightened her shoulders. "After he meets with

the management staff, I'm going to set him up in conference room three and bring them in one at a time."

Susanna nodded. Josie seemed to have everything under control. That was a relief. One less thing she had to think about.

When the two had left, Susanna turned to examine her office. Everything looked the same as when she'd left it the day before yesterday—except the door to the inner office was closed. For a moment, an unreasonable panic gripped her. Was the body still in there? Had the police merely closed the door and left it lying on the floor?

She shook off the macabre thought. No, of course not. No doubt the coroner had taken it away last night. Mr. Ingram was in a morgue somewhere, awaiting an autopsy.

Still, no harm in checking, was there? After all, she had to sit at her desk with her back to that door all day.

Her step across the carpet was slow. She reached for the knob but didn't touch it when she noticed the black smear all over the shining brushed metal. Fingerprint dust. She wrinkled her nose. Great. You'd think the police could clean up after themselves.

Grabbing a tissue from the box on her desk, she wiped off the powder, twisted the knob and pushed the door open a crack. Her gaze went instinctively to the floor where she'd seen the body last night. Empty. She released the breath she hadn't realized she'd been holding as she stepped into the room. An eerie silence dominated and made the emptiness more pronounced. Mr. Ingram liked to have a radio turned on low, playing country music.

She crept toward the desk. More black powder smudged the polished surface. Besides that, everything appeared to be in order. The desk held the normal things: a blotter, a pencil cup and wooden out- and in-boxes on each corner. Both stood empty. Mr. Ingram always cleared his desk before he went home at night. Tears threatened again as she thought of her boss performing his nightly tasks unknowingly for the last time.

She started to wipe off the fingerprint dust with the tissue, but stopped herself. Time enough to do that later. No doubt she'd need to go through his office sometime and box up Mr. Ingram's personal effects for his daughters, but today she had plenty to do at her own desk. She slipped out of the office and pulled the door shut behind her.

For starters, she needed to contact Mr. Ingram's attorney and ask what to do with the papers for the Corvette, which she was still carrying around in her purse. Then she had to call his oldest daughter, when it was a decent hour in California. Then she'd better find out when the board would like to set up an emergency meeting. Then… Better make a list.

She slid into her chair and leaned down to press the power button on her computer. Her gaze fell across the bottom file drawer of her desk. The catch had never worked properly, so she had to lift it slightly in order to close it. She did it by habit. But today the drawer wasn't latched. It protruded a half inch. She slid the drawer open and examined the contents. The files had been moved around. She always pushed them neatly to the rear of the drawer, but they'd been pulled forward.

Irritation set her teeth together. The police had searched her desk. What did they hope to find there? And they apparently didn't bother to put anything back in order when they were finished. Black dust everywhere, her drawer not closed all the way. What other evidence of their investigation would she come across?

"Uh, Susanna?"

A quiet voice from the doorway interrupted her thoughts. She looked up to see the head and shoulders of a tall young man peeking around the door frame, his body still in the hallway. Slender build, supershort haircut. That geeky guy from the computer department. What was his name? Justin something.

"Hi, Justin." She slid the drawer closed.

He eased into the room and stood just inside the doorway, hands clutching one another in front of his chest. "I, uh, wanted to say how sorry I am?"

Justin had an irritating habit of squeaking out the last words of his sentences so they sounded like questions.

"Thank you. It's a huge loss for all of us." There. She must be making progress. She'd managed to reply without tearing up.

His fingers intertwined, knuckles white. "I was just wondering if Mr. Ingram, uh…left me anything?"

Susanna arched her eyebrows. "Excuse me?"

Inside the gap of his unbuttoned collar, the knob in the front of his throat bobbed up and down. "We've been working on this project together? I don't know if he mentioned it?"

Actually, Susanna did remember her boss asking her to call Justin and have him come down to the office for meetings in the past few months. Something to do with a computer program, or the internet, or something. Mr. Ingram was always coming up with pet projects about which he became as enthusiastic as a little boy building a soapbox racer.

"He didn't leave any notes for me to distribute, and I just checked the out-box on his desk. It's empty." She formed her lips into an apologetic smile. "I'm afraid whatever project he had you working on will have to wait until a new CEO is appointed."

Crestfallen, the young man's shoulders drooped forward. "Okay. Well, thanks anyway."

He turned and slumped through the door. Susanna shook her head. Justin was an odd person. Apparently brilliant, though. Mr. Ingram had spoken highly of him on several occasions.

Her computer had booted up completely, so she pulled her keyboard toward her and began typing notes on her To Do list.

Jack stepped into the service box and bounced the ball a couple of times with his right hand while he settled his grip on the handle of his racquet with his left. His shirt clung to his body, soaked from the efforts of the first game. A drop of moisture tickled his face as it dripped from his forehead, and he raised his hand to wipe it away with a sleeve.

"It's not a basketball, you know. You're supposed to serve it, not dribble it."

He turned to spear his racquetball partner and long-time friend, Pastor Rob Collins, with a mocking grin. "You always get sarcastic when you're losing."

Sweat dripped from Rob's bangs. "Yeah, yeah, whatever. Just get on with it."

Jack bounced the ball twice more before he remembered he'd bounced before. Technically that constituted an out serve, but either Rob didn't notice, or he was prepared to let the error pass. Jack served the ball with as much force as his tiring muscles could muster, and Rob returned with even less energy. The rally lasted only a short while, then Rob took a dive and missed.

"My game." Jack extended a hand to his friend, who was beating his forehead dramatically against the polished floor. "And my match."

Rob used the hand as a lever to climb to his feet. "Enjoy the feeling. Next week I won't go so easy on you."

Jack laughed and fell in beside Pastor Rob as they headed for the locker room. The cardio machines they passed were all in use, the gazes of the evening exercisers fixed on the row of television screens suspended from the ceiling. He exchanged a nod with a couple of familiar faces.

"So, tell me more about this secretary." Rob grinned sideways at him as they entered the locker room.

Jack twisted the combination dial on his lock. "What's to tell? I did her a favor by storing her boss's car at R.H.'s for a few days, that's all."

"Hmm. You sure you aren't interested in her? You mentioned her at least a dozen times while we were playing."

What was this, a cross-examination? "That's ridiculous." Jack dialed the last number and jerked the lock open. "Of course I mentioned her. I was telling you what happened, and she was there."

Rob held up his hands as if to ward off an attack. "Okay, okay. I was just asking." He angled his racquet inside the locker. "Because if you *were* interested, that wouldn't necessarily be a bad thing, you know?"

Jack paused in the act of pulling out his gym bag to watch his friend through narrowed eyes. "You're not going to turn matchmaker on me, are you?"

"Of course not." His features screwed up for a moment. "But you know Carlye and I would like to see you find the same happiness we've found. Remember what God said about Adam. *It is not good for man to be alone.* We just don't want to see you end up—" He snapped his mouth closed on a word, then continued. "Alone."

Jack knew exactly what he'd been about to say. *We don't want to see you end up like your father.*

He avoided Rob's face by rummaging in the bag for the travel-size bottle of shampoo he kept there. "I learned my lesson the last time I asked a woman out. And the two times before that."

Rob's head dipped in acknowledgment. "You haven't had much luck when it comes to dating, I'll grant you that. But there are women out there who aren't interested in your money. You've just managed to zero in on the ones who are."

"It's a talent." He found the shampoo bottle, pulled out his towel and shoved the bag back in the locker. "Look, I know you mean well, but I've given this a lot of thought. I'm not in the market for a relationship right now. Women distract you from accomplishing your goals."

Rob opened his mouth to argue, but Jack cut him off with a raised hand. "My career stinks. I've got to give some serious thought about whether or not I'm going to stay in the family business, where obviously I don't have any real impact, or go somewhere else. I'm praying about that, but until I decide, a relationship would just be a distraction."

Disbelief crept over Rob's expression as Jack's words sank in. He shook his head. "I can't believe I'm hearing you say this. Women are a *distraction?*" He shook his head. "I hate to say it, but you sound just like your father."

"In this case, I think my father might be right." Jack shrugged. "I'm not saying I'll stay single my whole life. If God sends the right woman across my path, I'm open to that."

Rob studied him for a moment before a sad smile curled the corners of his lips. "With an attitude like that, how will you recognize her if He does?"

This conversation was becoming far too uncomfortable. Rob and he had been friends a long time, since their freshman year at the University of Kentucky when they'd visited a Campus Crusade for Christ meeting and accepted the Lord within days of each other. Jack had rejoiced with

Rob over his decision to enter the ministry, and wept with him over the loss of his dad a year later. Rob had been privy to Jack's frustrations with R.H. more often than he cared to count. But romantic advice crossed a line Jack wasn't willing to step over. Time to draw this conversation to a close.

He clapped his friend on the shoulder. "Tell you what. You have my permission to pray for God to open my eyes and shove me toward whatever woman He sends."

The sad smile became a grin. "Good idea. And I'm going to pray that He isn't gentle with that shove, because I want to enjoy watching you trip over yourself and fall flat on your face."

Later, Pastor Rob's question played over and over in Jack's mind. What if he was so busy trying not to become entangled in a relationship that he didn't recognize the right woman for him, even if God arranged for their paths to cross? What if, for instance, he'd already met that woman? Like…yesterday?

The sun had almost set by the time Susanna pulled into her driveway that evening. Poor Lizzie, who was normally one of the first kids to leave Miss Christy's house, had been standing alone at the living-room window, watching for her car to pull into the driveway. Susanna had felt a twinge of guilt when she caught sight of the anxious little face. There had been so much work to do at the office, and she'd gotten such a late start, that her watch inched past six o'clock before she realized the time.

"I'm hungry, Susu. Can we have pizza?" The question was delivered from the backseat with a whine, testimony to the normally cheerful child's anxiety.

Pizza was their traditional Saturday-night splurge after

a week of healthy meals. But tonight Susanna didn't have the heart to say no. "Sounds good to me."

Susanna switched off the car and slipped the strap of her purse over her shoulder. Lizzie extracted herself from her car seat and slid to the driveway when Susanna opened the door. A strong wind stung their cheeks as they hurried, hand-in-mittened-hand, up the short walk to the front door.

"Do you know what tomorrow is?" Susanna asked as she unlocked the front door and pushed it open. "It's Saturday. That means it's Cart—"

Shock snatched the words from her mouth. Instead of warmth from the furnace, she stepped into another blast of cold wind. Through the kitchen doorway, she spied the back door. It stood wide-open.

Someone had entered her house. Might even still be inside.

Without another thought, she scooped Lizzie into her arms and fled.

SEVEN

"I don't think there's anything missing in here."

Susanna shifted Lizzie's weight to the other hip as she surveyed the contents of the open "junk" drawer in the kitchen. The collection of miscellaneous items inside—rubber bands, a hammer and nails, a tattered owner's manual for the electric can opener—was in complete disarray, but they'd been that way before. The other drawers also appeared to be exactly as she'd left them, all except for the one containing the dish towels. The normally neat stacks of folded towels had been disturbed, though all were accounted for. After breaking the window in the back door, the burglar had apparently not spent much time in the kitchen.

Yet another new police officer—at this rate, she would meet every officer on the force by the end of the weekend—nodded and asked, "What about the bedrooms? Have you checked in there yet?"

"No, not yet," Susanna said. "I didn't want to go in there by myself."

She held down the childproof latch and slid the drawer closed. When the catch cleared the plastic, the distant echo of a thought hovered at the edge of her mind. Something about—

A loud knock on the front door interrupted the thought. Hefting Lizzie, she crossed into the living room and arrived at the same time as the police officer.

She opened the door to two people, and for a moment was too amazed to speak. Detective Rollins's presence made sense. She had insisted that the patrolman contact him immediately. But the man standing next to him surprised her. What in the world was Jack doing here?

"Ms. Trent." The detective dipped his head.

"Detective." She shifted her gaze to Jack and let her question show in her face. "Hi."

"I was on my way home from the gym and when I drove by, I noticed the police cruiser out front." His gaze slid behind her toward the policeman. "I thought I'd stop and make sure everything was okay."

Lizzie answered, her childish voice full of tears. "Somebody broke our door and stealed our stereo, the one we take on picnics."

Jack's eyebrows rose. "A break-in?"

Susanna nodded. "We discovered it when we got home."

"May I come in?" Rollins asked.

She stepped back and allowed them both to enter. As Jack crossed the threshold, he handed her a bundle of papers and flyers. "Your mailbox door was hanging opened, so I grabbed your mail for you on the way in."

"Thanks." Susanna shut the door behind them, tossed the mail on the coffee table and faced Rollins. "Did you hear about the incident in the middle of the night?"

He inclined his head. "I've read the officer's report."

"The people from last night must have come back, which means they probably weren't teenagers trying to find the keys to the Corvette for a joyride."

She looked at Jack for confirmation, and he nodded. "I moved the car this morning."

The detective's expression remained blank. "Let's not make any assumptions one way or another. It might still have been related to the Corvette, whether the car was on the premises or not."

Lizzie interrupted. "Susu, I'm hungry. When are we gonna call for pizza?"

"Soon, sweetie." She responded automatically without looking at the child, but stared at Rollins, trying to decipher his reasoning. "That makes no sense at all."

Jack cocked his head and studied Rollins. "I could buy curious teenagers getting a glimpse of that Corvette and coming back to steal it. But when they realized it wasn't here, why break into the house?"

Instead of answering, Rollins glanced at the uniformed officer, who stood listening a few feet away. "What did they take?"

"So far only small electronics. A portable CD player and a laptop computer. Ms. Trent hasn't checked the bedrooms yet."

Lizzie uttered a whiny sob and rested her forehead on Susanna's shoulder. "I'm hungry. Can I have a cookie?"

"Just a second, Lizzie." Susanna gave her back an absent pat, her attention focused on the detective.

Rollins gave a slight nod, as if the officer's words confirmed something for him. "Those are common items for thieves to target. They're easy to carry away, and easy to sell or pawn for quick cash. But it's possible the thieves expected to find something more." His eyebrows rose. "A person who has a classic car in their driveway may conceivably keep valuables in their house. We may not be dealing with teenagers, but my guess is the officer's assumption is correct. Last night's incident was precipitated by the presence of the car, and today the person or persons returned to see what else they could find."

That did make sense, and the explanation actually calmed Susanna's fears a fraction. "So you don't think either incident is connected to—" she paused, not willing to say the word *murder* in front of Lizzie "—Mr. Ingram?"

His answer wasn't the one she wanted to hear.

"I'm not ready to rule out the possibility." He switched his gaze to Jack. "I'll need to have a team take a look at that car, just to be on the safe side."

Jack's eyebrows had been drawn together as he followed the conversation. At Rollins's request, his brow cleared. "Of course. It's at my father's house in Hartland Estates. You can follow me there."

"It won't be me. I'll send a team over in, say," the detective said as he glanced at his watch, "an hour?"

Jack nodded. "Fine."

After he'd recorded the address in a pocket-size notebook, he switched his brief smile to Susanna. "I'll be in touch." Then he made his exit.

He certainly seems competent. The last time she'd trusted a detective to bring a criminal to justice, things hadn't gone so well. But Detective Rollins didn't look like a man who would cave in to bribery. *Besides, this is an entirely different situation. Relax. Let the cops do their job.*

Behind her, the officer cleared his throat. "Ma'am, I'll need to get a complete list of the items that are missing. I'd especially like to know about any credit card or checks. Those are likely to be used soon."

Susanna's grip on Lizzie tightened. "I hadn't even thought of that. Oh, no. I keep all my financial records in the bedroom."

She started for the hallway, but Lizzie was having none of it. The child began to wail.

"I'm hungry. I want pizza. You promised!"

Torn, Susanna halted and tried to calm the weeping girl. Susanna *had* promised. The poor kid was hungry, and frustrated, and probably frightened from all the trauma and disruption of the past twelve hours.

And yet, if the thieves had gotten her bank statements or credit card numbers, Susanna needed to contact the companies *now.*

Jack stepped forward and planted himself squarely in front of them. "Hey, you know what? Pizza is one of my favorite foods in the whole world."

Lizzie looked at him, her expression tragic, and the loud sobs softened. "It is?"

"Absolutely. And I was thinking maybe you and I could go in the kitchen and you can tell me what kind of pizza you like." He extracted a phone from his pocket. "We can call and order one together."

The sobs stopped completely, replaced by a heavily suspicious tone. "Who *are* you?"

Susanna bit back a sudden laugh at the bemused look on Jack's face. The question sounded so adult. Apparently all the lessons on not going anywhere with strangers had sunk in.

"His name is Jack," she told the child. "He's..." How should she describe Jack? They'd only known each other a short time, hours really. And those hours had been filled with trauma. And yet, somehow she felt she could trust him. The merest hint of heat threatened to warm her cheeks, and she couldn't meet Jack's gaze. "He's my friend."

Jack made a show of tapping on the screen of his phone. "My favorite pizza topping is broccoli, so if someone doesn't help me order, that's what I'll get."

Lizzie scowled. "That's gross."

He shrugged. "Well, then I need help deciding."

He extended a hand, and Lizzie paused only a second before she took it with her small one. Susanna set her down on the carpet. Not a hint of tears remained in the eyes the little girl turned upward. Susanna gave Jack a smile full of gratitude, and watched them disappear into the kitchen.

Lizzie's instructions about pepperoni and extra cheese followed her down the short hallway to the bedroom, where Susanna kept her financial files in a desk drawer. The child chattered like a chipmunk, apparently completely at ease with Jack. Amazing. The guy was handsome, helpful, friendly, had a steady job and was even good with kids. If only he weren't a billionaire, he'd be perfect.

"I hope your mommy's not mad at me for letting you eat dessert before supper."

Jack sat across a dinette table watching Susanna's daughter eat ice cream. The poor kid gulped it down as if she hadn't eaten in days. Judging by the speed at which the single dip of mint chocolate chip was disappearing, she would still have plenty of appetite left for pizza when it arrived.

"She's my Susu, not my mommy," the child informed him, speaking around her spoon.

Jack cocked an eyebrow. "Your Susu?"

Lizzie nodded, but didn't elaborate. Curiosity piqued, Jack cast about for a question to clarify their relationship. He had noticed Lizzie calling Susanna *Susu,* obviously a derivative of her name. Last night when he had checked the windows in the house, he'd seen the princess bedroom. The number of clothes hanging in the closet and toys overflowing the toy box bore evidence of constant use, not occasional. So Lizzie wasn't a periodic visitor; she lived here. Was Susanna the guardian of her younger sister, maybe?

He hadn't come up with a good question to ask the child when Susanna entered the room.

"I'm having ice cream." Lizzie held a spoonful in her direction.

"Mmm. That looks good. Can I have a bite?" Susanna stooped down and opened her mouth for the treat. She still wore the blue business suit, but the professionalism was somewhat diminished by the fact that she'd removed her shoes. Ten bright pink spots of color drew his attention to slender feet, and a couple of very shapely legs.

Jack cleared his throat and jerked up his gaze to her face. "Pizza's coming. Half cheese, half pepperoni, mushroom and black olives."

"And no broccoli." Lizzie gave her head a decisive dip.

"Whew. That was a close one." Susanna made a show of wiping her forehead in relief before slipping into an empty chair on the opposite side of the table from Jack. She turned a smile on him as she raised her hands to the back of her head. "Thank you for doing that. I appreciate it."

"No problem."

Jack had been about to explain that the pizza toppings had been Lizzie's idea because she knew that was what *Susu* liked, and they were his favorites, too, but the words got caught somewhere in the bottom of his throat. He couldn't look away from the waves of blond hair that tumbled free when she removed the clip that had held them confined. Surrounded by honey-colored strands, the eyes she turned his way took on a warm shade of light brown. He hadn't noticed her eyes before this moment, and now that he had, he couldn't speak.

She seemed oblivious to his silence. "They got my digital camera and some inexpensive pieces of jewelry, but those were the only things missing. They must have been in a hurry, because they didn't find the lockbox where I keep the few heirloom pieces my mother left me."

Shared loss sent a shaft of sympathy through Jack. Her mother had passed away, too, just like his. "What about the financial stuff?"

"Thank goodness they didn't take any of my checks, and I had my credit cards in my purse with me. I'm still going to alert the companies, though, just in case the thief wrote down the account numbers." She turned sideways in the chair and propped her feet on the edge of Lizzie's seat. "The officer said the fact that they took jewelry and small appliances supports the theory that these instances aren't related to, uh…" Her glance slid toward Lizzie, and then back to him. "Last night. Nothing was taken from the office."

The little girl was preoccupied with scraping the last bite of ice cream from her bowl.

Jack glanced at his watch. "I need to get over to my father's house and meet the cops who are going to search the car. They might need the keys."

"Oh." Her feet dropped to the floor. "You're right. They probably will. I'll get them from my purse."

Jack stood along with her. As he did, his gaze crossed the broken window in the back door. "Do you need some help with that? I can run by the hardware store after I leave the car and get something to secure it."

"Thanks, but I've already called an emergency window repair place. They should be here any minute."

An unexpected stab of disappointment struck him as he followed her into the small living room. He'd sort of looked forward to having a reason to return and maybe share their pizza. Which was ridiculous. The conversation with Rob after their racquetball game had certainly sent his thoughts down a strange path tonight.

From the corner of the sofa, she retrieved a purse that looked more like an overnight bag and began rummaging in it. To cover what might become an awkward farewell, Jack picked up the banded package of mail he'd retrieved from her mailbox earlier. He thrust it toward her as she held out a set of keys.

"Don't forget your mail. I noticed a priority envelope in there. Might be something important."

As she stared at the mail, questions flooded her eyes.

Great. Now she thought he'd gone through her mail. He started to stammer an explanation of how he hadn't been snooping, he'd just happened to notice, but the words stuck on his tongue.

What's the matter with me? I'm never tongue-tied.

She handed him the keys and took the bundle. A thick Priority Mail envelope lay at the bottom of the stack, beneath a couple of sales ads. She slipped the rubber band off and extracted it.

Jack jingled the Corvette keys in his hand. Time to get out of here before he made an idiot of himself. "Okay, I'm off. You have my number if you need anything, right?"

He took a backward step toward the door, but stopped when he saw the look on her face. Her lips parted and she lifted eyes as round as extralarge pizzas to him. All color drained from her cheeks.

"Is something wrong?"

Without a word, she held out the envelope for his inspection. Her name and address had been scrawled across the front in large, sweeping letters. Jack stared at it for a moment, uncomprehending. Then he noticed the return address. The package had come from Ingram Industries.

"I know that handwriting." Her whisper held the scratchy tone of someone who is teetering on the edge of shock. "It's Mr. Ingram's."

EIGHT

Susanna's hands trembled as she pulled the tab to open the flimsy cardboard envelope. She extracted a thin packet of loose papers held together with a paper clip. The one on top was a half sheet covered with Mr. Ingram's handwriting. She recognized the paper as coming from a notepad he kept in his desk drawer. Across the top read the words "From the desk of Thomas Ingram." There was no date.

Dear Susanna,

I know this is an odd request, but I'd like you to bring this package to work with you on Monday and return it to me. Tell no one about this! *I can't emphasize that strongly enough. From our years together I know I can trust you to honor my request. Your handling of confidential matters is one of the qualities I value so highly in you. I promise to explain everything in a few weeks.*

No doubt you think I've taken leave of my senses, but please humor a paranoid old man.

The letter was signed with a flourish, *Tom Ingram.*

She read the words a second time, her mind struggling to make sense of the request. *Odd* didn't begin to describe the bizarre arrival of a letter from her boss a full day after she had found his strangled body on the floor of his office. He must have dropped the envelope in the outgoing mail yesterday.

"What does it say?"

She raised her eyes from the script to find Jack studying her face. Should she tell him? Mr. Ingram had said to *tell no one*. But Mr. Ingram was dead.

Without a word, she handed him the packet. His eyebrows inched up his forehead as he read. "Wow."

"Do you think he knew someone was coming to his office to look for these papers?"

"That's my guess, and he didn't trust whoever it was." He flipped through the papers clipped to the note. "Take a look at this."

Susanna stepped to his side to examine the top page. Two long creases, pressed flat now, indicated that the paper had been folded like a business letter. At the top of the page was the number "1," then a gap followed by a list of random typewritten words and numbers, double-spaced.

120
By Fair Play
5k
Hisself
6x Over Upset
Fly Without Wings
Abaft

"Abaft?" She raised her gaze to Jack's. "What does that mean?"

"I don't know."

His expression proved he was as baffled as her. He lifted the page, and Susanna saw a second sheet with an identical format, but different words and numbers. They made no sense, either.

Jack flipped through the packet. "The number at the top of each is apparently a page number. There are ten of them."

Something settled inside the Priority Mail envelope. Susanna slipped her hand inside the flimsy cardboard. When she pulled out the items inside, she drew in a small gasp.

Two small canvas pouches with drawstring openings cinched shut. Just like the one in the Corvette's papers.

She held them in the palm of her hand toward Jack. "I know what's in these."

While he opened them, she snatched her purse off the couch and pulled out the plastic envelope containing the packet she'd received from the auction.

"Look at this." She uncinched the pouch and dumped out the coin-shaped token inside. "I figured it had something to do with collectible cars, like a proof of purchase. But I guess not."

Jack picked up one of the tokens from the envelope with a thumb and forefinger. "Number four. And the other is number seven." He stared at token number nine in her hand a moment. "Hold on a second. What if—"

His mouth shut on the words as he flipped through the stack of papers Mr. Ingram had sent her. She watched his eyes move as they scanned the page.

"Yeah, that makes sense." He jerked a nod, and then grinned up at her as though she knew exactly what he meant.

"What makes sense?"

"They're clues." He tapped the page with a finger. "Cryptic clues, like a crossword puzzle. See, look at page number nine."

He held up the sheet of paper for her inspection.

80
Blood Red
Warship
9756 Original
Top Dollar Wins
L-48
Sister Tamale

As Susanna read, the bewildering words began to make sense. "*Blood Red*. That's how Mr. Ingram described the color of the Corvette he wanted me to look for. And *80* is the year the car was manufactured." She squinted, her mind racing. "*Top Dollar Wins* could refer to an auction."

"Yeah, I'm sure it does." Enthusiasm made Jack's words come faster. "Not many people know that the word *Corvette* actually means *warship*. And I remember looking at the information sheet in the window. The horsepower was listed as L-48, and there were 9756 original miles on the engine."

Those all made sense, but Susanna stared at the last clue on the list. "*Sister Tamale?* Because tamales are red, maybe?"

"Good guess, but I don't think so. Tamale is a city in Ghana, and it's actually one of Louisville's sister cities."

"And Louisville is where we went to the auction." She stared at him, amazed. "How do you know that?"

"Oh, I know a lot of useless facts." A grin creased Jack's mouth. "But in this case, there's a sign listing the sister cities just inside the city limits of Louisville, and I happened to read it when I was driving to the auction."

The smile was so appealing, so little-boyish, Susanna couldn't help returning it. The tickle in her stomach acted as a warning sign, an unmistakable signal of a blossoming attraction. What was that all about? She absolutely would *not* get involved with someone like Jack. Never again would she make a monumental mistake like that.

She wiped the smile from her face and lowered her gaze to the papers. "So apparently Mr. Ingram solved the clues on pages four and seven, and found those tokens. Then he sent me to get number nine. I wonder who came up with the clues?"

Jack shrugged and slipped tokens four and seven back in their pouches. "I guess that's for Detective Rollins to figure out."

Startled, her gaze flew back to his face. "We can't give these to the police."

Now it was Jack's turn to look surprised. "Why not? They might be important."

She stared at the familiar script on the note. Mr. Ingram's warning weighed on her. She could almost hear his voice instructing her to *tell no one*. He'd made a point of stating how important it was to keep the contents of this packet secret. He trusted her to keep his confidence. Though he was dead, Susanna owed the man more than she could ever repay. When she had first interviewed for the job as his secretary, she didn't have nearly the experience required to assist the president of a large corporation. And she was desperate for a job, a means of supporting herself and then eighteen-month-old Lizzie. She'd landed the interview for pity's sake, because her father had worked for Ingram Industries before the tragedy that took his life. And maybe that same pity was the reason Mr. Ingram hired her. Regardless, she'd always done the best she could to make sure he never regretted the decision. She would be forever grateful, and she'd do whatever she could to honor his request.

Besides, who knew better than she that not all police officers were on the up-and-up?

"I—I don't think this had anything to do with his death." She took the papers from Jack's hand and slid them back inside the envelope. "I spoke with his attorney on the phone this afternoon, and he's going to send someone to the office on Monday to pick up the Corvette papers. I'll let him decide what to do with these, too." She held out her hand for the tokens.

Jack shook his head as he handed them over. "I don't think that's a good idea."

Would he say something to the detective himself? He was on his way to meet the police so they could search the car. Could she trust him to keep his mouth shut? No, of course not. She'd learned long ago that she couldn't trust anyone but herself. If only she hadn't opened the envelope while he was still here, or showed him Mr. Ingram's note.

But it was too late now. The only thing she could do was try to convince him to keep Mr. Ingram's secret.

"Please, Jack. Don't mention this to the police. Let me turn them over to the attorney. He'll know how to handle the situation."

A struggle showed on his face. Susanna watched, her breath caught in her chest. Finally, he relented.

"All right, if you're sure that's what you want to do."

Relieved, Susanna released the breath. "Thank you." *Who knows? Maybe he keeps his promises.*

She tucked the Priority Mail envelope into her purse with the car papers. Mr. Ingram's attorney was the right person to handle this. She'd feel a lot better when the tokens and all these strange clues were in the hands of someone official.

* * *

Two vehicles arrived as Jack steered his truck away from the curb in front of Susanna's house—a pizza delivery car and a van with the logo *AA Glass Repair* in large letters across the side. The sight of both eased the odd protective twinges that had plagued him from the moment she had opened the door to him and Detective Rollins, a clearly distraught Lizzie propped on her hip.

What is going on, Lord? If this is because of Rob's prayer for me to meet a woman, I'd just as soon You wait a little while before answering that one, okay?

He glanced at the dashboard clock as he executed the turn out of Susanna's neighborhood. R.H. rarely left the office before eight o'clock, which left about forty-five minutes for the police to get there, conduct whatever search they needed to perform and leave before the elder Townsend arrived. Jack didn't even want to think about R.H.'s reaction if he came home to find police cruisers lining his driveway.

Why didn't Susanna want to turn the tokens over to the police? Loyalty to her late boss, no doubt. It had probably been a mistake to agree with her request not to mention them. Rollins needed to know about them. Of course, if Ingram's attorney was worth his salt he'd know that, and insist that she give them to the detective.

But what if they really were a clue to Ingram's death? What if they could somehow identify his killer? Even worse, what if the killer knew about them? Rollins's warning to Susanna last night might prove to be true.

Jack's hands tightened on the wheel. Yeah, that promise had definitely been a mistake. But he'd made it, and something in him stopped him from betraying Susanna by going back on his word. So he'd just have to keep a close eye on her between now and the time she released that package into the custody of the attorney.

The prospect wasn't entirely unpleasant.

Jack pushed that thought away. Best not go there.

As he neared R.H.'s house, the clues on those papers marched across his mind's eye, a parade of random words and numbers. Only they weren't random, obviously. Each one fit with the others somehow, filled a place in an overall whole that meant something. The pattern might not be discernable at first, but that just made finding it more intriguing. Like a half-finished crossword puzzle, the empty places screamed to be filled, the clues to be solved.

There had to be a pattern to the clues, a detectable style which the writer adopted unconsciously. When he'd first started working crosswords, the clues had seemed just as cryptic as the ones in Ingram's packet of papers, but after a few, he'd begun to find the writer's technique in each puzzle. That made solving them much easier.

The same was probably true here. The clues on page number nine all made perfect sense, now that he knew the token had been hidden in the Corvette's papers. From those obscure descriptions, he could get a glimpse of the way the clue-writer's mind worked. For instance, a person who described a *Corvette* as a *warship* liked to find obscure facts and little-known definitions of words. So Jack could apply the same thought process to the clues on one of the other pages. How would that same mind come up with those other words and numbers?

I can impress Susanna when I solve all those clues.

With a start, Jack realized the turn his thoughts had taken. He immediately wiped the smile from his face. What was that all about? He didn't need to impress anyone. And he didn't need to keep thinking about Susanna, either.

He cranked up the volume on his radio and focused his attention on the road.

Long before the Disney movie ended, Lizzie had fallen asleep on the couch still wearing her thick robe and fuzzy bedroom slippers. Susanna covered her with a blanket and tried not to envy her. She considered turning off the DVD to watch something targeted at adults for a change, but then the good part of the cartoon came on. Though she'd watched it a million times with Lizzie, she couldn't press the stop button until she'd seen the prince and princess smiling into each other's eyes and they set off on their happy ending.

If only life really worked that way.

Her cell phone rang as the music swelled to its final crescendo. She pressed the power button on the remote control with one hand and picked up her phone with the other. The number was vaguely familiar, but no name came up.

"Hello?"

"Hey. I hope I'm not bothering you. I just wanted to check in and see how you two are doing."

Jack. A rush of pleasure warmed her insides at the sound of his voice.

The reaction irritated her. She had no business being happy to hear Jack's voice. Instead of allowing herself to settle comfortably against the padded arm of the couch, she straightened her spine and sat rigid.

"We're doing well." She forced all warmth from her voice and instilled her words with the polite professionalism she used at work. "It's been a quiet night."

"Good. Did Lizzie enjoy her pizza?"

Susanna glanced at the sleeping child beside her. "Yes."

She could elaborate, tell him how Lizzie ate two pieces of cheese pizza even after the ice cream. How the child had chattered for an hour about her "new friend Jack." Could have thanked him again for distracting Lizzie while she dealt with the police. But if she said any of those things, that would be an invitation to step deeper into their lives. She couldn't risk that.

After a brief pause, Jack said, "The police didn't find anything in the Corvette. They took some fingerprints, but they didn't expect them to lead to anything."

"You didn't tell them about the package, did you?" The question came out sharper than she intended.

"Of course not. I promised, didn't I?"

Susanna closed her eyes. "Thank you."

"So what are you two doing tomorrow?"

"Uh…" Why was he asking? Surely he didn't want to hang around with them. "I've got a list of errands to do." Not a complete lie. She did have a list, but it consisted of grocery shopping and cleaning the bathroom. And trying to keep her mind off the recent horrible events. "Weekends are pretty busy around here."

"What about Sunday? Maybe we could go to lunch after church or something."

Ah. He's a church guy.

She allowed herself to relax against the couch cushion. That made her determination not to get involved much easier. If she ever did decide to get involved with a man again, not only would he not be rich, he definitely wouldn't be involved with a church.

"Thanks, but I don't think so."

Before he could reply, a beep sounded in Susanna's

ear announcing an incoming call. She pulled the phone away to check the screen. A local number, but not one she recognized.

"I've got another call coming in, Jack," she told him.

"Okay. I'll talk to you soon. Bye."

What did he mean by *soon?* She would have asked, but he hung up before she could get a word out.

Pushing Jack out of her mind, she answered the incoming call.

"Hello?"

"Who am I speaking with?" The voice on the other end was muffled by a bad connection or something, the words barely understandable.

For some reason, the hair on the back of Susanna's neck prickled to attention. Telephone safety rule number one: *never give your name or address to a stranger over the phone.*

"Who were you trying to call?"

"Susanna Trent, secretary to the late Mr. Thomas Ingram, of Ingram Industries."

Okay, the man knew who she was. This was obviously a business call. Maybe a reporter. The public relations manager at work had warned her that the press might contact her and other employees for a statement. But how did whoever-it-was get her personal cell phone number?

"This is Susanna Trent."

The next words were like an icy finger trailing up her spine.

"I know you have token number nine. I want it."

NINE

Everything became clear with breathtaking clarity. How naive she'd been to assume the tokens and Mr. Ingram's death weren't connected. Of course they were. Only an idiot would think otherwise.

Fear pressed like a weight against her chest, reducing her breath to short, shallow gulps. Lizzie stirred beside her on the couch. Afraid the sound of her voice would awaken the child, Susanna slipped off the cushion and crept away. She didn't speak until she reached the kitchen.

"I—I don't know what you're talking about."

"I think you do. The token isn't in the Corvette, so it has to be with the papers."

This was the man who had searched the Corvette. Not teenagers out for a joyride. A man looking for a coin-size token.

Pleading ignorance might be a stupid ploy, but it was the only one she could come up with at the moment. "Token? What token?"

"I have neither the time nor the patience to explain it to you. I need token number nine. If you haven't found it yet, check the papers that came with the car. I assume you still have them."

He *assumed* she had the papers, which meant he didn't

know for sure. She needed to stall, give herself time to think.

Ask a question. Keep him talking.

"Are you the one who broke into my house?" A more fearful question hovered behind that one. *Did you kill Mr. Ingram?*

He didn't answer. "I don't want the papers, just the token. Hand it over and you'll never hear from me again. But if you choose to be uncooperative…"

The threat hung in the air, unspoken but undoubtedly present. Her knees began to tremble. Should she hang up right now and dial 9-1-1? Or maybe she should call Detective Rollins. Tell him all about the tokens and the papers, everything.

As if he had a microphone hidden in her brain, the man on the phone said, "If you're thinking of calling the police, you might want to think again. If you do, Ingram Industries will close its doors within three months."

Susanna sank against the kitchen counter to keep from falling. "What do you mean?"

"When Tom Ingram's criminal activities are exposed, his reputation will be destroyed and his company will collapse. You and all the other employees will lose your jobs."

She didn't believe it. Mr. Ingram was an honest, upstanding man. He'd never do anything to put his company in jeopardy.

At least, she didn't *think* he would.

The words from his note hovered into focus in her mind. *Tell no one about this!* Could he have been doing something illegal?

"What illegal activity? What was he doing?" The questions slipped out before she could school the doubt from her tone.

When the man answered, she heard triumph in his voice. He knew she wouldn't willingly endanger Mr. Ingram's reputation, or his business, which meant he had the upper hand. "Just put token number nine on your back porch and go to bed. When you wake up in the morning, this will all be behind you."

Her back porch? He was planning to come to her house tonight, slink around in her backyard with her and Lizzie asleep in bed? Correction, not asleep. She'd never be able to sleep knowing the owner of this creepy, muffled voice was stalking through her yard. Why hadn't she chopped down those big, overgrown evergreen shrubs that bordered her rear and side yards? Some misguided idea of privacy without paying for a fence. Why didn't she realize they just created a hiding place for robbers and murderers?

She had to say something to keep him from coming here. "I—I don't have the papers. I wasn't kidding. They're not here. They're…" Where? Her thoughts floundered. What could she say that didn't sound like a lie? "They're at the office, along with all Mr. Ingram's other belongings."

Don't tell lies, Susie. She could almost hear her mother's voice echo across the years from childhood. *They always come back to haunt you.*

"Then go get them."

Mama was right. Now she was trapped. Either she'd have to admit her lie, and that she had the token here, or she'd have to take a trip to the office in order to support her story that it was there. She tried to imagine herself carrying Lizzie from the parking lot of Ingram Industries down the long sidewalk beside those dark, frozen woods, and utterly failed. She couldn't leave the safety of her house.

Why hadn't she turned everything over to the police, like Jack wanted?

"On second thought, don't go get the token tonight," the

muffled voice said. "The police are probably watching the building, and a car in the parking lot this late at night will draw unwelcome attention. Besides, I have another task for you."

Her hands were damp with sweat. "A task?"

"Ingram told me that he had other tokens. I need them all. So bright and early tomorrow you will go to the office, get token number nine, and search for the others. If you don't find them, go to his house and search there. Nobody will question your presence at either place. I'll call you before noon and let you know what to do with them."

Susanna's shaking knees could no longer support her weight. She slid down the kitchen cabinet to the floor. Was she supposed to become an errand girl for her boss's killer?

When she didn't answer, the muffled voice spoke again. "I sense your hesitation. Remember, if you go to the police about the tokens, you'll expose something much bigger than you can possibly imagine. But if you turn them over to me, this will all go away. By this time tomorrow, life will return to normal. Make the right decision, Susanna."

At the sound of her name uttered by his voice, her stomach gave a queasy lurch. There was something terrifyingly personal in hearing her name from the lips of a killer.

And what if she refused? The envelope in her purse seemed to flash like a beacon from its hiding place in the next room—not five feet away from where Lizzie slept. If she didn't do what this man said, would they become his next victims?

Agree to it. Anything to get him off the phone. Then I can think.

"Okay." Her voice almost failed her, and she had to swallow before she could continue. "I'll try to find them in the morning."

The line went dead without an acknowledgment.

Violent shaking overtook her body. Susanna wrapped her arms around her knees and hugged them tight, unable to get up off the cold kitchen linoleum.

Could it be true? Was Mr. Ingram really involved in something criminal? Much as she didn't want to believe that of him, how else could she explain his insistence in his note that she tell no one about the tokens? There seemed no doubt at all that the tokens were somehow responsible for his death. And if what the man on the phone had told her was true, they could be responsible for destroying everything he had worked to establish. They would rob his daughters of their inheritance, and hundreds of employees of their jobs, including Susanna.

Suddenly she hated those tokens, hated the very thought of them. They were like…like fire, raging out of control and destroying everything it touched. Killing those she loved. She and Lizzie had experienced enough destruction in their lives. The sooner she got rid of those tokens, the better. Then she and Lizzie would go someplace safe and fun and far away from here.

But she couldn't give them to a killer. Even if it meant she and all the other employees at Ingram Industries lost their jobs, she couldn't make herself do that. *Not even for you, Mr. Ingram*. In the morning she'd call the attorney, and she and Lizzie would take the package over to his house. He'd know what to do.

Her trembling subsided enough that she managed to climb to her feet. Like she'd done the night before, she wedged sturdy chairs beneath the front and back door-knobs. Then she gathered Lizzie in her arms and settled the child in her bed for the second night in a row before securing the bedroom door with another chair.

* * *

After he hung up from talking with Susanna, Jack waited over an hour for his father to come home. The temperature in the truck cab plummeted, and he burned a quarter tank of gas by starting it repeatedly to warm himself with the heater. Seemed ridiculous to sit in the driveway instead of going inside since this was, after all, the house where he'd grown up. The family home. But he'd come away from their conversation at the office today knowing that he was no longer welcome to think of this as *his* home. How had R.H. put it? "You have your own place. Don't offer *my house* as a storage facility." Couldn't get much clearer than that.

Several times he considered calling Susanna back, but then grew angry with himself for trying to fabricate an excuse to talk to someone who obviously didn't want anything to do with him. He went over his conversation with Rob at the racquetball court a couple dozen times, and ran the gamut from admiring his friend's courage to dismissing him as a meddling busybody.

He did not pray. If God was giving him the shove Rob said he planned to ask for, and if that shove was toward Susanna, then Jack wasn't in the mood to talk to Him, either.

Finally, when he couldn't stand another minute with himself and his racing thoughts, the lights inside the garage came on and the door began to rise. R.H.'s car pulled into the driveway a second later.

"About time," Jack muttered as he climbed out of the truck's cab. Where had the old man been until almost nine-thirty at night, anyway?

R.H. stood waiting beside his car when Jack rounded the corner and entered the garage.

"What are you doing here?" His question held a trace

of the hostility that had become the hallmark of every conversation they held lately.

Jack worked to keep his tone pleasant. "Just wanted to talk to you for a few minutes."

R.H. studied his face through narrowed eyes, then snorted. "Come in, then. But I have to make a call to California at ten."

Jack followed him into the house and through the kitchen to the family room beyond. Nothing had changed since his boyhood. Every stick of furniture was exactly the same, and in exactly the same place it had always been. Immaculate, of course, thanks to the cleaning lady who came in three times a week. Once during his teen years, Jack had wondered if his father's refusal to change anything at home was his way of creating a shrine to preserve his dead wife's memory. But soon he realized it was nothing of the sort. R.H. simply didn't care enough to change anything. His attention was focused on his company, not on his house or anything in it—including his children.

Jack lowered himself to the leather sofa in front of a big stone fireplace facing his father's armchair. Neither of them settled comfortably in their seats. Instead, Jack imitated R.H. and perched on the edge of the cushion, his spine rigid, both feet on the floor.

Before the silence could become awkward, Jack asked, "Have you been at work all this time?"

He knew the question was a mistake the moment it left his mouth. R.H.'s chest puffed out with a hiss of indrawn breath.

"Some of us actually have to work to keep that company running. We don't run out the door at five-thirty to play games."

Jack ignored the accusation. "If there's a project I can

help with, I'll be glad to do it. I'd love to get involved in whatever you're working on."

R.H. studied him for a moment. Was he actually considering giving Jack some meaningful work, something besides maintaining supply contracts that had been in place for decades?

His father dashed his hopes with a single sentence. "Richard's got it under control."

Of course he does. Because my own father doesn't trust me. He still thinks of me as a kid.

R.H. planted his elbows on the arms of his high-backed chair and intertwined his fingers. "I've got things to do tonight. What do you want to talk about?"

During his hour in the driveway, Jack had considered the best way to approach the subject of the tokens. That R.H. knew something about them, Jack was certain. Why else send him to buy the Corvette? The man wasn't in the habit of buying cars at auction. When he'd first handed the auction brochure to Jack and instructed him to buy the Corvette, Jack had wondered if his father was finally planning to have a little fun. He'd pictured R.H. zooming around the curvy country roads outside Lexington in the red sports car, wind ruffling his thinning hair.

But with the discovery of the token in the car's papers, Jack knew his assumption had been wrong. Ingram and R.H. were after the same car because they both wanted that token. There could be no other explanation. Which meant R.H. knew something, and it might be important.

No sense pussyfooting around R. H. Townsend. He could detect a stall in an instant, and it just made him irritable. The best approach was always the direct one.

"What's going on with those tokens?"

Rarely did Jack have the opportunity to see his father rendered speechless. The man's mouth dropped open, and his neck extended a few inches like a turkey's. An expression of utter disbelief slackened the muscles in his face.

And then the moment was gone as though it had never been. R.H.'s mouth snapped shut and his eyes narrowed. "What are you talking about? I don't know anything about any tokens."

The denial irritated Jack. Did his own father really think he was stupid? For once, he didn't bother to filter emotion out of his words. "I think you do. You never wanted that Corvette. You just wanted the token that came with it."

"You're not making any sense."

But the statement sounded false, a feeble attempt to maintain a deception that Jack knew was slipping out of R.H.'s grasp.

Not often did Jack get the upper hand on his father in any conversation. He pushed his advantage. Time to show R.H. that his son knew more than he gave him credit for. "And that's not the only token, either. There are ten, along with clues to the location of each."

R.H. had spent years developing a closed businessman's face, but tonight he seemed to have dropped the mask. Jack watched the thoughts play across his face, his eyes grow distant for the seconds it took him to consider Jack's words, and then focus again.

He leaned forward, his palms gripping his legs just above the knees. "You don't know what you're talking about."

"I don't know it all, but I know enough." Jack was enjoying having the upper hand. "I've seen three of the ten tokens."

R.H. blinked. A moment later he launched himself out of the chair and rounded the coffee table that separated them. He stood in front of Jack, forcing him to tilt his head back to look up at him.

"Listen to me. The stakes are high in this game. I'm

telling you right now to forget anything you think you know. Don't mention it again, to me or to anyone else."

Jack found it hard to look away from the intensity in his father's eyes. "But if these tokens have anything to do with Ingram's death, the police need to know."

His eyebrows came crashing together below a forehead heavy with creases. "Of course it doesn't have anything to do with Ingram's death. That's a ridiculous suggestion."

"But the t—"

R.H. cut off Jack's argument with the slice of a hand through the air. "We're not going to have this conversation. Take my word for it, there's no possibility that Tom Ingram's death is related in any way to this." He glowered into Jack's face. "I mean it, Jack. Don't talk about this to anyone. Don't even think about it anymore."

With that, R.H. stomped out of the den. A moment later, Jack heard the door of his study slam shut.

He sat there a moment, considering possible actions. He could do as his father demanded—go home, go to bed and put the tokens out of his mind. Or he could follow his father and demand more information. No, that would be fruitless. In his almost thirty years, Jack had never known R.H. to back down from a decision, particularly when he'd stated it that strongly.

There was always the option of contacting the police. But something in his father's insistence made him hesitant. Besides, he'd promised Susanna.

That was an idea. He could call Susanna, the only other person in possession of all the same pieces of information he had.

The grandfather clock in the hallway began to chime, a sound he'd heard every hour for as long as he could remember. Ten o'clock. Too late to call Susanna tonight. First thing in the morning, then.

He made his way to the back door, his sneakers silent on the gleaming hardwood floors. At the door to the study, he paused. The drone of his father's voice filtered through the heavy wood, the words indistinguishable. The call to California, where Townsend Steakhouses was planning to open its newest restaurant. R.H. had probably already put the conversation with his son out of his mind and returned to business.

Nothing new there.

Susanna awoke when she turned over and instead of the soft pillow, her cheek touched the sharp edge of the book she'd been reading when she fell asleep. The last thing she remembered was checking the clock around three and wondering if she would ever be able to get a good night's sleep again. She cracked open one eye to check the time. Seven-sixteen. Well, four hours were better than none.

Beside her, Lizzie had snuggled beneath the thick comforter and wrapped her body around a pillow. Only the top of her curly head was visible. Moving slowly, Susanna pulled back the comforter so she could look at the sleeping face. Fine blue veins lined her eyelids, and her sweet little bow-shaped lips moved in sleep as if to pucker for a kiss.

Susanna stopped herself from brushing her fingers through the tousled curls. The sun would be up soon, and Lizzie shortly afterward. She might as well take advantage of the time alone to get her shower. Then, while Lizzie was eating her cereal and watching Saturday-morning cartoons, she'd call the attorney. Beyond that, she didn't know. Their actions today depended on what the attorney recommended.

Moving slowly so as not to jostle the sleeping child, she slipped out of the bed. She grabbed a pair of jeans and a sweater from the dresser, then slid the chair away from the door. Having that heavy object wedged beneath the knob really did make her feel better. But someday Lizzie would have to go back to her own bed. Maybe she should look into an alarm system.

She left the bedroom door open in case the little girl woke up while she was in the shower, and tiptoed down the hallway to the bathroom. Minutes later, Susanna stood beneath the showerhead while rivers of hot water warmed her skin. Why were her muscles so stiff this morning? Tension, probably. She hadn't really been able to relax since the moment she stepped into Mr. Ingram's office Thursday night. Steam rose around her while she allowed the water to wash away the tension. The shower felt so good she stood there longer than usual, until the small, steam-filled bathroom began to feel like a sauna.

Dried and dressed, with her hair piled in a towel on top of her head, she stepped into the hallway. The house was still quiet. The sun had risen while she showered, though only a gloomy pale light peeked around the edges of the curtains in the living room. Must be a cloudy day. She half considered letting Lizzie sleep, but if she missed her favorite eight o'clock cartoon, she'd be upset.

"Lizzie, guess what time it is? It's time for Doodle-bops."

When Susanna stepped into the bedroom, the first thing she noticed was the temperature. Her skin, warm from her shower, erupted with chills.

The second thing she noticed was the empty bed. Lizzie was not there.

TEN

Time stuttered, and Susanna's heart along with it. The floor was clear, so Lizzie hadn't fallen out of bed. Had she woken up and gone into her own room? Yes, that had to be it. Her robe and slippers were missing from the foot of the bed. They'd been there twenty minutes ago, when Susanna left to take her shower. She whirled and crossed the short hallway in two steps.

Lizzie's bedroom was empty, the princess bedspread undisturbed.

"Lizzie? Where are you?" Her voice, shrill with alarm, filled the small house.

No answer.

She ran to the living room, where the front door was still barricaded shut with the chair she'd put there last night. The room was deserted. Same thing with the kitchen door.

"Lizzie!"

The only answer was her own sharp voice echoing off the walls.

Lizzie was gone. Panic rose from her stomach to claw at her chest.

But how? The doors had not been opened. In a flash, she remembered the cold air in the bedroom. The window.

She ran to the room and jerked away the curtains from

the double window that looked out on the backyard. It stood open. The screen was gone. Outside, a completely white sky cast a dull, lifeless light over her empty backyard. Behind the thick bushes that bordered her property lay a small public park. When she bought this house, it had initially seemed an ideal place to raise a child. Now she knew it was nothing but an escape route for vandals.

The police. She had to call 9-1-1. They'd put out an Amber Alert or something. Surely here the police weren't crooked. And even if they were, this wasn't a politically sensitive case, like the one in Tennessee. This was a missing child.

She ran from the window to her nightstand and snatched up her cell phone. Her fingers froze on the keypad when she caught sight of the note on Lizzie's pillow. A single white sheet of paper with typewritten words.

Do not call the police. If you do I'll hurt the girl. Believe me. Wait for my call.

Nausea mingled with the terror in her stomach. Lizzie was her whole life, all she had left. Without her, there was no reason to go on living. Susanna might as well curl up and die. Her legs folded, and she crumbled to her knees on the floor beside her bed, the phone in one hand and the note in the other.

"Help me. Please help me."

The prayer fell from her lips almost unconsciously. She had no faith that God heard it. Or if He did, that He would answer. The last time she had asked God to save someone she loved, her prayer had been ignored. But what else could she do? This was bigger than she could handle by herself.

Believe me, the kidnapper had written. She did. If

she called the police, he would hurt Lizzie. She couldn't risk that.

Still, she had to call someone or she would go insane. Mr. Ingram's attorney? No. Last night he'd been the right choice to later turn the tokens and papers over to, but this morning, with Lizzie in the hands of a killer, he was too official, too much like the police. She had no family except Lizzie, no close friends who could be trusted to help her keep a level head in a situation like this.

What about Jack? He'd been at her side when they found Mr. Ingram's body. He knew about the tokens, had figured out that the random words on the papers were clues to their locations. And he'd been so nice to Lizzie last night, so compassionate and friendly. Could she trust him? Maybe not, but what choice did she have? If she didn't call someone, she'd go insane.

Her hand shook so violently she had to hold her wrist still with the other one before she could see the Received Calls list on the phone screen. She found his number and tapped it twice. The phone started to ring.

"Hello?"

"Jack?" A sob squeezed her throat shut, and for a moment she gave in to noisy, shuddering breaths.

"Susanna?" Alarm sounded in his voice. "What's wrong? Are you okay?"

"I need help," she managed to whisper between sobs.

"I'm on my way."

The moment Jack walked through Susanna's door, a hysterical woman threw herself into his arms. Sobs racked her body, and for several moments he could do nothing but hold her and let the storm run its course. Her hair hung in damp tangles down her back and made a wet spot on the shoulder of his T-shirt where she pressed her forehead. Any minute he expected to see Lizzie peek around a corner to investigate what caused her Susu to cry like this, but the child was nowhere in evidence.

Like a blow to the gut, he realized how unusual that was.

He enclosed Susanna's arms in his hands and held her back so he could see her face. "Has something happened to Lizzie?"

Still unable to do more than cry, she nodded.

"What's happened? Where is she?"

She gulped, and finally got a few words out. "She's been k-kidnapped."

Shock pounded him like a boxer's fist. "Kidnapped?" The word sounded foreign on his lips, something you heard about on television. Certainly not applicable to anyone he knew. "When? What happened?"

"Fifteen minutes ago." She handed him the crumpled sheet of paper she clutched. The words blazed from the page into his brain.

"Have you called 9-1-1?"

When she shook her head, he reached for the pocket of his jeans. He hadn't touched his cell phone yet when she shrieked.

"No!" She grabbed his arm and jerked it toward her. "He says he'll hurt Lizzie if we call the police."

Hysteria pierced into his ears through her voice. He had to calm her down or she was going to have a heart attack or something.

"Susanna, listen to me. Kidnappers always say that. They want you to think you're all alone, that you have no option except to do what they say. But the police can help. They have people who've been trained to handle situations like this."

Were the Lexington police trained to handle kidnappings?

He had no idea. Maybe they'd contact the state police, or even the FBI. He didn't want to admit that his knowledge of police procedure was limited to what he learned from television shows.

Susanna's head shook so forcefully locks of her wet hair stung his face. "I'm not trusting Lizzie's safety to a bunch of hostage negotiators."

He infused his voice with a calm, soothing tone. "I think you should reconsider. We're talking about a desperate criminal. You and I are not equipped to deal with someone like that."

She took the note from his hands and stepped backward. Her chest shuddered once more before she mastered the sobs. "I've thought about it. Whatever they ask for, I'll pay it. We don't have a lot of money, but I'll beg if I have to."

Money? Was that what this was about? Angry flames licked at the edge of his thoughts. Was that why she'd called him instead of the police, because she thought he would pay the ransom for her? So much for thinking he would ever mean anything to any woman except a fat bank account. And so much for Rob's prayers.

You'd think a pastor's prayers would hold a little weight.

With an effort, Jack doused his anger until it receded to a dull flicker of resentment. This called for a clear head. Of course Lizzie's life was worth any amount of money. But kidnappers never followed through with their end of the bargain once they had the money, did they?

He combed his fingers through his hair and scrubbed his scalp, trying to clear his thoughts. "It's not that I'm not willing to pay whatever it takes to get Lizzie back, but I really think we need to get help from someone who's equipped to deal with a situation like this."

Susanna stared at him as though he was speaking a

language she'd never heard. Then her features cleared as understanding dawned. "You think I'm asking you for money?" She shook her head. "No, that's not why I called you. Lizzie's father has money. Or her grandfather does, anyway." She buried her face in her hands, and her next words were muffled. "They don't even know about her birth, but I'll tell them if I have to. I'll call them as soon as I know how much it will take to get her back."

Jack digested that information. Susanna's child, who called her *Susu* instead of *Mommy,* came from a wealthy family that didn't know she existed. The revelation opened so many questions, but now was not the time for them.

Instead, he asked, "Then why did you call me?"

Her features crumpled as she surrendered to tears again. "I—I just needed a friend."

Something tight in Jack's chest broke free. He opened his arms and she stepped into his embrace. The tears that poured through her this time came not from hysteria, but from somewhere deep inside.

Jack hugged her tight and whispered, "Shh. It's going to be fine. We'll figure it out."

He had no idea how, but at that moment he knew he'd do whatever it took to help Susanna get Lizzie back.

At the ring of a cell phone, she jerked away to snatch the phone off the coffee table. Round eyes raised toward him after she examined the screen.

"It's him."

"All right." Jack put a steadying hand on her back. Her body trembled beneath his fingers. "Try to be calm. Ask to speak to Lizzie. Tell him you want to make sure she's okay."

Was that right? He had no idea, but that was what they did on television. It sounded like a good idea to ascertain that the child was safe and healthy and—he gulped—alive.

Susanna nodded, swallowed and pressed the button to answer the call. "Hello?"

Jack stood beside her. He could hear a man's voice but couldn't make out the words, which meant he'd have to wait until Susanna hung up to find out the details. In the meantime, he'd do the best thing he could do for her. He'd pray.

He began to do just that.

"You didn't call the police, did you?"

The words were fuzzy, just like last night. One part of Susanna's brain realized that this wasn't just a bad connection. He must be masking his voice somehow.

"No, I didn't call the police." She looked at Jack, who nodded to encourage her. "I want to talk to Lizzie."

Jack's eyes were fixed on her, but his lips moved silently. With a start she realized he was praying. *Good. Maybe God will listen to his prayers.*

The voice on the phone rasped against her eardrums like a loathsome, scaly reptile. "In due time. First, I expect you want an explanation."

From the time she realized Lizzie was gone, Susanna's thoughts had been frantic. Why would a kidnapper take a child? To get money, of course. What other reason would there be? But now she remembered the topic of her conversation with this man last night.

"It has something to do with the tokens, doesn't it?"

"Very good. When we talked last night you didn't seem very committed to finding them for me. Now you have some motivation."

He had kidnapped Lizzie because of those stupid tokens? "I have three. I'll bring them to you right now. Just don't hurt Lizzie. Please."

"Three? Which ones?"

"Seven, four and nine. Mr. Ingram sent them to me in the mail the day he died, along with ten pages of clues."

A pause. "You lied to me."

The words were soft, indistinct. But they sent a chill up Susanna's spine.

"I...I was afraid. I didn't want you coming to my house again." She clutched the phone in a hand gone suddenly damp. "I'll put them on the back porch right now, like you said. Just bring Lizzie home."

"I don't think so. Three isn't enough."

A knot lodged in her throat, and her next words were delivered on a sob. "But that's all I have. That's all Mr. Ingram sent me."

"Then you have work to do. Don't waste your time on five or eight. Get the rest of them, and you can have your daughter back."

"What?" A thick fog of panic enshrouded her brain, and nothing made sense. She shook her head to clear it. "When will I get Lizzie back?"

"When you find the rest of the tokens." He paused. "Are you good at solving riddles?"

Susanna pressed backward against Jack's hand, trying to somehow draw strength from his touch. "No, I'm not. What if I can't find any?"

"That would be a shame. She's such a pretty little girl."

Horror marched across Susanna's arms on thin, hairy legs. "Don't hurt her," she whispered.

"That's entirely up to you. Find the tokens, and she'll be fine. Just as she is now. Here. Listen for yourself."

A scratching on the line, and then the voice she longed to hear said, "Susu? I don't like it here. Will you come get me?"

Lizzie's childish voice wavered with fear, just like it

had a few months ago when Susanna made her sit on Santa Claus's lap for a picture. Pain stabbed Susanna in the heart. Oh, how she longed to grab the child and take her far, far away from anything that frightened her.

Crying on the phone wouldn't help Lizzie. It would only frighten her further. Susanna gulped a fortifying breath and, with an effort she didn't know she possessed, choked back her tears enough to speak normally. "Soon, sweetie. I promise, I'll do everything I can to come get you soon. Are you okay?"

"I had a doughnut." Susanna could almost see her little chin trembling with her effort to be brave. "I can have another one when we get there, if I don't cry."

The line crackled and rubbed against something, and then the muffled voice returned. "You have until tomorrow night at nine to recover the rest of the tokens. Do that, and she'll be returned to you safely. I'll call you later for a progress report."

"But what if I can't find them?"

His voice dropped. "Oh, I hope you can. I really do."

The menace in his words chilled Susanna to the core. She couldn't squeak out a response.

"One last thing. Call the police, and you'll be signing her death warrant. And just to prove that I mean business, check your back porch."

The line went dead.

The back porch? What could he have left to convince her that he'd hurt Lizzie if she didn't comply? Dread bloomed in her chest like an expanding bloodstain. Still gripping the phone in her hand, Susanna leaped off the couch and dashed into the kitchen.

Jack followed on her heels. "Where are you going?"

"He told me to check the back porch."

Jack jumped ahead of her to jerk the chair from beneath

the doorknob, and she fumbled with the lock for a moment, her fingers clumsy. Finally, she threw open the door and ran out onto the back porch.

At first, she thought it was empty. Then she spied a rectangle of white on the edge of the concrete. An envelope. The kidnapper had written another note? She scooped it up and, fingers trembling with fear, lifted the unsealed flap.

"What is it?" Jack asked.

Not a piece of paper inside. Susanna tilted the envelope and emptied the almost weightless contents into her palm. For a single moment, her brain didn't identify the object. And then she realized.

In her hand lay a thick, golden curl from Lizzie's head.

Susanna doubled over and gave in to sobs.

ELEVEN

"You're sure Lizzie sounded okay?"

Jack sat beside Susanna on the couch, watching her rifle through the pack of papers from the Priority Mail envelope with unsteady fingers. The hysterical weeping had finally passed, but he'd rather see tears than this frantic activity. She was stretched to the breaking point, and she wouldn't be able to keep her sanity if she went on like this.

Her nod was jerky. "She sounded scared, but she wasn't crying. She said he promised her a doughnut if she didn't cry." Her lips screwed up as she fought a wave of emotion, and then she went on in a rush. "She loves them. We don't have them very often, because of all the sugar. Her favorite is chocolate, the kind with icing, but any doughnut will do."

The babble stopped when Jack gathered both of her hands in his. Her fingers were icy, and he set about warming them with a gentle rubbing.

"We're going to get her back." He leaned forward and caught her eyes with his, forcing her to look at him. "Do you hear me? We're going to do everything we can to get her back."

Her throat contracted with a spasm, and then she nodded.

"Do you have any idea how he got in?" Jack pitched his voice low and even.

"Through the back window in my bedroom while I was in the shower. The glass wasn't broken, though." She clenched her hands together, her knuckles white. "I don't think it was unlocked, but I—I didn't check it last night."

Jack had gone through this house window by window the night before last. He'd inspected every single lock. "I'm positive that window was locked when I dropped off the trailer Thursday night. If this is the same person who broke into your house yesterday, I'll bet he unlocked the window to give himself an easy way to return." He pounded a fist on the arm of the couch. "I should have checked them again last night."

She placed a hand on his arm. "It's not your fault, Jack. I'm just so glad you're here."

The touch of her fingers on his bare skin, combined with the emotion he heard in his voice, did funny things to his insides. His resolve to get Lizzie back became even stronger.

The two of us can't do this on our own, Lord. We need some heavy-duty help.

"I want you to know I still think the best thing we can do is contact the police." Panic flooded her eyes. She opened her mouth to speak, but he cut off her protest. "However, I respect your decision not to. So, that means it's up to us and God. Now, the only instructions this madman gave you was to solve the clues and get the tokens. Right?"

She managed a tremulous smile of thanks, then nodded. "That's right. Oh, and he said not to bother with five and eight. I guess that means he already has them."

Jack released her hands and picked up the papers on the coffee table. He removed the note from Ingram and slid it, along with the paper clip, inside the cardboard envelope with the three tokens.

"So, we have number four, number seven and number nine." He extracted the corresponding papers out of the stack and set them aside. "He has number five and number eight." Those two pages joined the others. "Let's see what that leaves us."

The remaining five pages in his hand, he sat back on the couch. Susanna settled in beside him, and together they examined the list of words and numbers on the first page.

After a moment, she shook her head. "None of that makes any sense to me." She covered her face with her hands. "This is hopeless."

"Now, wait a minute. I did some thinking about this one last night."

She peeked at him from between her fingers. "You did?"

"Yeah." True, worrying about his father had occupied more of his time than these clues, but he had thought about them a little after he got home. "I looked up the word *abaft*. It's a nautical term that means *to the rear of*."

"I didn't even realize it was a real word." She ran a finger down the list. "Do any of these others mean anything to you? What do *120* and *6x Over Upset* mean, for instance?"

"I don't know for sure," Jack admitted. "I couldn't remember all the other clues. But I have a feeling I know what *Fly Without Wings* means. Have you ever been out to the Kentucky Horse Park?"

She twisted sideways on the cushion to look at him. "Only once. I took Lizzie to see the Christmas lights."

"Well, right inside the visitor's center there's a gigantic mural above the doors. It shows a herd of wild horses galloping through water. It's really beautiful, which is why I remember it so well. The caption at the bottom reads *Thou Shall Fly Without Wings*. They also show a video with the same title."

"So you think token number one is at the horse park?" Her shoulders inflated with momentary hope, but then sagged. "That's a huge place. It will take forever to find a token there."

Jack held up a finger. "Not if we look at the rest of the clues. For instance, if you know much about thoroughbreds, you know they're identified by their parentage. But instead of saying, 'He was sired by Fair Play' some people in the thoroughbred industry say, 'He's *by Fair Play*.'" He tapped the words with his finger. "One of the greatest horses in the history of racing was Man O'War, and he was *by Fair Play*."

Excitement lit a fire in her eyes. "He's buried at the horse park, isn't he?"

"Sure is. There's a big statue right beside the visitor center." Jack ran his finger down the rest of the clues. "I don't know what most of these other clues mean, but I think that's a good place to start."

"What are we waiting for? Let me grab some shoes."

Susanna was out of her seat in a flash. While she went to retrieve her shoes, he gathered all the papers and stuffed them into the envelope. They'd better keep these with them, just to be on the safe side.

Moments later she hurried back into the room pulling a comb through her hair. When she'd twisted it in a quick ponytail at the back of her head, a knock sounded on the door.

She tossed a startled glance at him, and then crossed the room toward the door. Alarm raced along Jack's nerve endings. What if this was the killer, returning boldly to

HOW TO VALIDATE YOUR
EDITOR'S FREE GIFTS!
"THANK YOU"

1. Peel off the FREE GIFTS SEAL from front cover. Place it in the space provided at right. This automatically entitles you to receive two free books and two exciting surprise gifts.

2. Send back this card and you'll get 2 Love Inspired® Suspense books. These books have a combined cover price of $11.00 for the regular-print or $12.50 for the larger-print in the U.S. and $13.00 for the regular-print or $14.50 for the larger-print in Canada, but they are yours to keep absolutely FREE!

3. There's no catch. You're under no obligation to buy anything. We charge nothing—ZERO—for your first shipment. And you don't have to make any minimum number of purchases—not even one!

4. We call this line Love Inspired Suspense because every month you will receive stories of intrigue and romance featuring Christian characters facing challenges to their faith and their lives! You'll like the convenience of getting them delivered to your home well before they are in stores. And you'll love our discount prices, too!

5. We hope that after receiving your free books you'll want to remain a subscriber. But the choice is yours—to continue or cancel, anytime at all! So why not take us up on our invitation, with no risk of any kind. You'll be glad you did!

6. And remember...just for validating your Editor's Free Gifts Offer, we'll send you 2 books and 2 gifts, *ABSOLUTELY FREE!*

YOURS FREE!
We'll send you two fabulous surprise gifts (worth about $10) absolutely FREE, simply for accepting our no-risk offer!

Steeple
Hill®

The Editor's "Thank You" Free Gifts Include:

- Two inspirational suspense books
- Two exciting surprise gifts

YES! PLACE FREE GIFTS SEAL HERE

I have placed my Editor's "thank you" Free Gifts seal in the space provided above. Please send me the 2 FREE books and 2 FREE gifts for which I qualify. I understand that I am under no obligation to purchase anything further, as explained on the opposite page.

About how many NEW paperback fiction books have you purchased in the past 3 months?

❏ 0-2   ❏ 3-6   ❏ 7 or more

E9FT   FC4P   FC4Z

❏ I prefer the regular-print edition   ❏ I prefer the larger-print edition
123/323 IDL   **110/310 IDL**

Please Print

FIRST NAME

LAST NAME

ADDRESS

APT.#   CITY

STATE/PROV.   ZIP/POSTAL CODE

Offer limited to one per household and not applicable to series that subscriber is currently receiving.

Your Privacy—The Reader Service is committed to protecting your privacy. Our Privacy Policy is available online at www.ReaderService.com or upon request from the Reader Service. We make a portion of our mailing list available to reputable third parties that offer products we believe may interest you. If you prefer that we not exchange your name with third parties, or if you wish to clarify or modify your communication preferences, please visit us at www.ReaderService.com/consumerschoice or write to us at Reader Service Preference Service, P.O. Box 9062, Buffalo, NY 14269. Include your complete name and address.

▶ Detach card and mail today. No stamp needed. ▶

© 2010 STEEPLE HILL BOOKS PRINTED IN THE U.S.A.

LISUS-EC-11

The Reader Service —Here's How It Works:

hurt Susanna? He leaped toward the door and stepped in front of her.

"Let me open it," he told her.

She hesitated only a moment, then nodded and stepped back.

Jack braced his foot against the floor three inches inside in case someone tried to push in the door, and straightened his spine until he stood his full menacing six feet. Then he cracked open the door just enough to peek through.

The last person in the world Jack expected to see stood on her front porch.

Detective Rollins.

Susanna stepped back when Jack swung the door wide. The sight of the detective almost made her sob. For one hopeful second she'd expected to find Lizzie on the other side of that door.

Rollins stared into Jack's face for a long moment, his thoughts completely masked behind an impassive expression. Then he dipped his forehead in a greeting.

"Mr. Townsend." His gaze slid to her face. "Ms. Trent. I have some good news."

Hope mushroomed in her chest again in an instant. But the next moment it evaporated. His news couldn't have anything to do with Lizzie. He didn't know about the kidnapping.

And he couldn't know.

She speared Jack with a meaningful glance that she hoped he interpreted as, *Don't tell him anything,* and then forced a smile for Detective Rollins. "Good news? Did you discover something about Mr. Ingram's death?"

"I'm sorry, no." His eyes moved as he glanced into the room behind her. "May I come in for a moment? Unless I'm interrupting something."

"Oh, no. Nothing. We were just going—" Her mind went blank. She speared Jack with a panicked look.

"Out to brunch," he finished for her, then stepped back to allow Rollins inside. "But we can wait a few minutes."

Susanna marveled at Jack's nonchalance, and tried to match his tone as she followed the detective a few steps into the living room. Rollins stopped in front of the couch and looked at her expectantly, obviously waiting for an invitation to be seated. She didn't offer one. Her nerves were like tightropes stretched from the top of her head to the soles of her feet. He needed to say whatever he came to say and get out of there, so they could get to the horse park and find token number one.

Jack closed the front door and joined them. "Is the news about the break-in?"

"That's right. Ms. Trent's things were recovered in a trash can in the park behind the backyard."

Things don't matter. I want to recover Lizzie.

But she smiled and said, "That's wonderful."

Rollins's lips pursed and twisted sideways. "It's also strange. Why go to the trouble to steal a laptop and camera and jewelry, and then dump them?"

"Maybe they got nervous," Jack said. "They were afraid to get caught, so they got rid of the evidence."

Rollins studied Jack's face for a long moment. "That's possible. There's another possibility, though. What if the thief took those things only to lend credence to the break-in theory? What if he or she had another reason for entering your home?"

Like searching for tokens, or unlocking a window so he could come back later and kidnap Lizzie?

Susanna fought to keep her tone even. "I don't know what other reason anyone could possibly have."

"You're sure nothing else is missing? Something from Ingram Industries, perhaps?"

She returned his stare without blinking. "I don't bring work home."

Jack spoke. "Maybe the thief wasn't after some*thing*. Maybe he was after some*one*."

Susanna shot a poisonous glare at him. He promised not to tell!

He ignored her and continued to look at Rollins. "Ms. Trent is a very attractive woman." His cheeks pinked, and he cleared his throat. "What if someone broke in here with the intent of attacking her, and then lost his nerve? He might grab a few easy-to-carry things to make it look like a robbery."

The detective's lips twisted back and forth as he considered. "Possible," he finally pronounced, "but not probable. That theory doesn't take into account the Corvette or Ingram's murder."

Susanna stopped herself from looking at her watch. *How much longer is he going to stay? They must get going.* Another thought occurred to her, a horrible one. *What if the kidnapper drives by and sees a police car in my driveway? He'll think I called the police, and he'll hurt Lizzie.* She had to get rid of Rollins quickly. If only she had something to give him, something to keep him busy and off their backs while they tracked down Lizzie.

The solution came to her in a snap. "Wait a minute. There is something that ties the Corvette and Mr. Ingram to my house." She snatched up her purse and rummaged in it for the plastic envelope containing the car papers. What difference did it make if she turned them over to the police? She and Jack had the token.

She produced the package and handed it to Rollins. "The papers I got at the auction when I bought the Corvette.

Maybe the thief was looking for them. That's the only thing I can think of."

To her immense frustration, he opened the plastic envelope, extracted the papers and began paging through them. Did he plan to examine every one on the spot while precious time slipped away, second by second?

Jack slipped a hand around her to rest on the small of her back. The gentle pressure he exerted felt steady, strong. She glanced at his face and saw the message in his eyes, in the nearly imperceptible upward twitch of his mouth. *Stay calm*. She drew in a long breath and relaxed her clenched fists.

Rollins fanned the pages, then slipped them back inside the plastic. "Do you mind if I take these with me?"

Thanks to Jack's steady hand on her back, Susanna was able to smile and reply calmly. "I'm sure that'll be fine. I'll let Mr. Ingram's attorney know you have them."

The detective's stare became penetrating. Susanna endured the scrutiny and assumed what she sincerely hoped was an innocent expression.

After a few seconds that felt like hours, he released her gaze. "Good. On Monday you'll need to go down to the evidence room at police headquarters and positively identify your property."

"I'll do that."

She opened the door for him, but did not follow him outside. On the porch, he turned to look at her.

"If there's anything else you think we need to know, you'll call?"

Susanna looked him directly in the eye. "Of course I will." *As long as it doesn't endanger my Lizzie.*

After another long moment, he gave a nod. "Goodbye, Ms. Trent." He switched his gaze to Jack. "Mr. Townsend."

When he started down the porch steps, Susanna closed the door with extreme care behind him. When it snapped shut, she turned and collapsed against it.

TWELVE

During the twenty-minute drive down Interstate 75 to the Kentucky Horse Park, Jack tried to occupy Susanna's mind by having her read the other clues to him. If they were able to find token number one, that would give him an even better feel for the clue-writer's thought process. He had a vague idea of the location of number two, though he didn't say anything.

"Rear View of Justice? What does that mean?" Susanna dropped her face into her hands. "It's no use. We'll never find them all in time."

Jack laid a hand on her arm. "Don't lose hope. We've just started searching. I have some ideas about a couple of those clues."

"You do?"

The hope in her tone evicted a more confident reply than he would normally have given. "Yes. We're going to figure them out."

He didn't give voice to his primary worry, because that would push her over the edge. What if they found all the tokens, but the kidnapper killed Lizzie anyway? A recurring theme in the cop shows on TV was not to negotiate with kidnappers because they never kept their word. Was that true in real life? Reports of all the terrible things done to abducted children paraded through his mind.

This case had one unique twist that gave him hope. The tokens. This kidnapper obviously wanted those tokens badly, and that might give them the edge they needed to get Lizzie out of this alive. They had to discover the purpose of the tokens, and the identity of anyone who knew of their existence.

And there was one person who knew more than he had admitted.

With one hand on the steering wheel, Jack edged his cell phone out of his pocket and speed dialed his father's office. No answer.

That's weird. He's always at the office on Saturdays.

Next, he tried the home phone, and again received no answer. He didn't really expect R.H. to answer his cell phone, because he rarely turned the thing on unless he was going out to the hunting lodge, which had no landline. As he expected, that call went straight to voice mail.

Beside him, Susanna raised reddened eyes from studying the clues. "Who are you calling?"

"My father, but he's not answering." He glanced sideways at her. "I think he might know something. Last night I asked him why he wanted that Corvette so badly, but he wouldn't give me a straight answer."

Her hands clutched the shoulder strap that cut across her collarbone. "Do you think he knows about the tokens?"

"He denied it but…" A picture of R.H.'s wide eyes last night surfaced before his mind's eye. "Yeah, I do."

"Then call him back." Her voice filled the truck cab. "Force him to tell us what he knows."

Jack tried the office line again, but still received no answer. Maybe R.H. was on another call, or in a meeting with someone. Much of the office staff worked on

Saturdays. He left a message asking his father to call him back about an urgent matter, and then left a similar message on the home answering machine.

"Jack, look."

Susanna indicated something on the side of the road. It took him a moment to realize she was pointing toward the exit sign. Iron Works Pike, the road that would take them to the Kentucky Horse Park, was clearly marked Exit *120*.

"Well, that's another clue explained." He switched on the turn signal. "It proves we're on the right track."

A smooth two-lane driveway wound through the park. A few horses stood in the wide-open pastures lined by plank fencing. Winter had turned summer's deep green bluegrass a dingy gray, which was apparently unappetizing. The horses they passed stood on the frozen ground, but did not graze.

Jack parked the truck in the visitors' center lot. Only a half-dozen vehicles were scattered around the lot. Low attendance for a Saturday, probably due to the cold weather. They made their way between pillars of white stone. An arch atop the golden seal of the Commonwealth welcomed them to the Kentucky Horse Park. Despite the cold, a flock of geese stood knee-deep in the trickling stream that ran through the park. They crossed a stone bridge toward the visitors' center. Susanna skirted around statues of foals, heading toward the doors, but Jack stopped her.

"The Man O'War grave site is this way."

He pointed to the left, then guided her down a wide path toward the circular alcove that had been built to honor the famous thoroughbred. A waist-high stone wall surrounded a large planter, and a life-size statue of Man O'War himself stood in the center. They approached the statue and stood facing the bronze replica. Thorny, winter-bare rosebushes filled the planter in a ten-foot circle around the horse's feet.

Jack scanned a sign at the entrance to the circle. "Take a look at this." He pointed at the gold lettering that detailed basic statistics of the horse's life. "Man O'War sold at auction as a yearling for five thousand dollars."

Susanna grasped the page containing the clues for token number one in her hands. "One of the clues is 5K."

Jack nodded. Moment by moment he was becoming more certain they'd found the location of one of the tokens.

Susanna read from the paper. "We know what *120* means, *Fly Without Wings* and *By Fair Play*. What about the rest of them?"

They moved past the sign to approach the statue. Jack eyed the bronze replica. "If *Abaft* means *to the rear*, then the token may be hidden in the rear part of the statue. But I don't see where. It looks solid."

He circled the wall slowly, scanning the figure for a hole or a crevice, anyplace big enough to hide a coin-size object. The bronzed tail hung down several feet, and was crafted with creases and folds like real horsehair. There might be a hollow beneath the upper part, where the tail met the body. Hard to tell from this angle. He glanced behind him. Though he could see no other visitors in the vicinity, a couple of groundskeepers were working near the corner of the visitors' center, not more than fifty yards away. A sign on the planter clearly stated *Please Keep Off.* If the groundskeepers noticed him hopping up on the wall and running his hands over the statue, they'd be here in a heartbeat.

Susanna had moved in the opposite direction to inspect the other side of the statue. "Jack, look at this."

He came around the circle to join her before one of

several plaques mounted to the wall, each giving facts of Man O'War's career as a thoroughbred racehorse. This one talked about his second year, and described an incident where an amazed spectator watching him race asked, "Who's he by?" and someone replied, "He's by hisself, and there ain't nobody gonna get near him."

"Hisself," Jack said. "Another clue solved."

"And look here." Susanna pointed at another paragraph on the plaque. "The only race Man O'War ever lost was to a horse named Upset, but later he went on to beat him *six times*." Excitement sparkled in her eyes. "That's the last clue explained—6x Over Upset."

Jack shot a glance toward the groundskeepers. They hadn't moved. Maybe if he worked quickly he could get up there before they noticed.

"I'm going to check out the rear of that statue," he told Susanna.

"Abaft," she said.

He nodded, and circled around to angle the bronze figure between him and the men. The informative plaques were mounted on the concrete wall by means of a frame, so they protruded like slanted tables for easy reading. Jack approached the one behind the statue. This was the point closest to the tail. He could hop up on the wall here, directly behind the tail, and—

A thought struck him.

He paused with his foot in midair. "Wait a minute. That's not it."

Susanna hurried to join him. "What isn't it?"

Jack stared up at the statue and let the thought take shape. "*Abaft* doesn't mean *to the rear*. It means *to the rear of*."

Understanding dawned in her eyes. "So the token is *behind* the statue."

Jack nodded. *To the rear of* the statue inside the planter were rosebushes. The token might be buried in the soil there, but he didn't think so. It would be too easily found or exposed. Instead, the hiding place must be somewhere more secure. He angled himself directly behind the statue's tail, and followed a straight line to...

The plaque in front of him. It consisted of a sturdy metal shelf bolted to the concrete wall. He ran a hand over the sides of the frame. His fingers grasped the edge and curled around it. The shelf was hollow. He dropped to his knees and peered beneath.

"Bingo."

Long strips of duct tape attached a small object to the bottom of the shelf. The tape held fast. He had to work at it a second to peel it away, but when he did, he uncovered a canvas drawstring pouch identical to the three they already possessed. A sense of grim satisfaction settled in him as he removed the tape from the pouch.

"Got it."

He handed it to Susanna, who emptied the token into her palm.

"We have number one." The eyes she raised toward him shone. "Thank you, Jack. You did it."

The temptation to bask in her appreciation was strong, but they didn't have time to pat themselves on the back. Jack acknowledged her thanks with a quick smile, then gestured toward the park exit.

"Come on. We've got four more tokens to find."

Back in the truck, Susanna added token number one to the envelope containing the others. The jubilation of finding another token faded before they even reached the parking lot. Lizzie's life was in jeopardy, and every time

Susanna looked at her watch more precious minutes had passed.

What if that crazy man hurts her?

Fear clawed at her, and for a moment the daylight around her darkened with visions of her precious Lizzie lying on the office floor where Mr. Ingram's body had been.

A choking sound escaped her clogged throat. In the next moment, frightened sobs filled the truck cab.

In an instant Jack's arm was around her shoulders, his hand squeezing strength into her. "We'll find the rest of them. We just have to get into this guy's head, that's all. But you have to hold it together. We've got to be clear and focused."

The truth of his words penetrated her fearful thoughts. She gulped back the tears. This wasn't helping Lizzie.

"You're right," she said when she could talk again. "Sorry. It's just that I can't stand the thought of…" She swallowed and stared at her hands. "Lizzie is all I have. And I'm all she has. If anything were to happen to her, I don't know what I'd do."

He twisted in his seat so he was facing her. "You mentioned her father earlier." He held up a hand. "You don't have to tell me anything you don't want to, but I wondered if maybe he should be notified. Maybe he can help."

Bitterness rose with a flood of acid in her throat. "Trust me, if the kidnapper had asked for money, I would have called him in an instant. All he's good for is writing a check."

Jack's eyebrows rose. "But if he knew his daughter was in danger, surely he would help."

"I won't call him."

The anger in her voice seemed to ricochet off the windshield. Susanna winced when she heard herself. Had she become so bitter against Bruce that she would endanger Lizzie's life just so she didn't have to talk to him again?

She placed a hand over Jack's and squeezed an unspoken apology. "I'm sorry. Bruce is a sore subject, one I usually avoid discussing."

"Understood. I won't mention him again."

He turned the key in the ignition and the truck roared to life. Susanna snapped her seat belt buckle as he backed out of the parking space and headed for the main road. From the corner of her eye, she studied his profile. Why was he helping her? Until two days ago, they had never laid eyes on each other. When she had first heard his name and realized the connection to billionaire R. H. Townsend, she'd dismissed him as a self-centered playboy, just like Bruce. Instead, he'd proven himself to be anything but. He'd shown kindness after kindness to her and to Lizzie, even when she had treated him coolly.

She owed him an explanation. No, she *wanted* to explain, wanted him to understand about Lizzie. About her.

"Lizzie isn't my daughter, she's my niece," she blurted out.

No surprise registered on his face. "I knew she had to be closely related. I thought maybe she was your sister."

"My sister's daughter. Marti was only seventeen when she got pregnant with Lizzie. I was twenty-one, working as a secretary for a small company in Tennessee, and Marti came for a visit. She'd never met my fiancé."

Painful memories flooded back. Susanna stared out the window at the road zooming past beneath their tires. Why hadn't she kept closer tabs on Marti during that terrible weekend? She'd been so stupid, so trusting.

"Your fiancé?" Jack's voice was gentle.

She nodded. "He was in college, and we met at a friend's house. We weren't going to tell our parents about the engagement until Christmas, but Marti and I told each other everything, so of course she wanted to meet him." She rubbed her thumb across the empty place where her engagement ring had been. "We went to a party, and Bruce said he was going to introduce his new little sister around. I guess he'd had too much to drink." She closed her eyes and tried not to picture the next part, the part that hurt so badly to think about.

When she opened them, Jack's hands were clenched on his steering wheel, as though bracing himself for what came next.

"Marti was afraid to tell me." She gave a short laugh. "She didn't want to hurt me. But when she realized she was pregnant, she finally did."

"Well, I hope that guy paid through the nose." His words were infused with barely controlled fury.

"Oh, that's the best part. I confronted him, and Bruce didn't bother to deny his guilt. He offered to pay for an abortion." Her fingernails bit into the flesh of her palms. "When I threatened to have him arrested for rape, I got a visit from the chief of police. He advised me to take the offer and let the matter drop."

Jack turned his head to level a look of disbelief on her. "He paid off the police?"

She didn't filter the bitterness out of her voice. "His father was quite wealthy, and didn't want the publicity. And besides, Marti was ashamed and just wanted to put the matter behind her. She refused to identify the baby's father to anyone, even our parents, and she swore me to secrecy, too. She talked about giving up the baby for adoption." She smiled at the memory of newborn Lizzie moments after birth, her tiny face red beneath a shock of fuzzy blond hair. "But we were all glad she didn't."

"So how did you end up with Lizzie?"

Susanna couldn't look at him as she answered. "Marti and our parents died when Lizzie was eighteen months old. The house burned down." The familiar lump lodged in her throat. "Dad died in the fire. Marti and Mom lived for a few days, but…" She shook her head. "Lizzie was the only survivor."

His hand snaked across the center console to cover hers. "I'm so sorry."

Silence settled between them. His hand offered a warmth of comfort, and she accepted it from him gladly. How different he was, filled with strength and tenderness in equal parts. Bruce would never have—

With a jerk, she arrested the thought. Jack was nothing like Bruce. To compare them, even in her thoughts, was an insult to the man who was helping her get Lizzie back.

She faced him. "So you see why I don't want to call Bruce. I doubt if he would help in the first place. But what if he finds out he has a daughter and decides he wants her? With the backing of his father's money, he might take her away from me." She shook her head. "I can't risk that. When she's old enough, I'll let her make her own decision about contacting him."

Jack veered the truck off an exit heading toward town. Susanna watched Jack's profile as he processed the details she'd just given him. She'd never shared those details with anyone before, and she found herself waiting for his words.

Jack rolled the truck to a stop at the bottom of the exit ramp. The face he turned toward her held a determination that helped to soothe the fear that gnawed at Susanna's stomach.

"We're going to get her back." Not even a hint of doubt.

Susanna allowed herself the first real smile since the

horrible moment when she came into the empty bedroom. "Thank you."

The light changed, and Jack turned the truck left onto a busy street. Three lanes of traffic flowed in both directions past the large shopping mall where Susanna had taken Lizzie to visit Santa Claus just a few months before.

"Where are we going?" she asked.

"To get the second token, I hope." He glanced in his rearview mirror before changing lanes. "I'm not entirely sure about all the clues, but I think I know at least two of them."

She picked up the envelope and pulled out page two to read the clues. "*First King, Treasure Hunter, Glowing Reflection, Amid Glass and Amber, Signed in Chocolate* and *Bovine in Pink*." She shook her head. "None of those mean a thing to me."

"How well do you know your Bible history?"

Bible? Susanna twisted her lips. "Not at all."

A question lurked in the quick look he shot in her direction. Susanna avoided his eyes. She'd done enough talking today without going into the whole God thing.

Thank goodness he didn't push the matter. "Israel's first king was named Saul."

She ran a finger across the first clue written on the page. *First King*. The answer came to her. "Saul Good Restaurant & Pub."

"I've only been there once, but I remember they have a chocolate bar, which might have something to do with the chocolate clue." He flipped on the turn signal. "The only thing is, there are two Saul Good restaurants, so we have a fifty-fifty shot at getting the right one."

He turned the corner and steered the truck into a busy open-air shopping center. Buildings lined both sides of the street, and the cars of Saturday shoppers filled the parking lots.

Susanna scanned the clues again. The last one snagged her eye. *Bovine in Pink*. A memory surfaced. A cow in a pink dress. A birthday party she'd taken Lizzie to.

She looked up from the page. "We have the right one. Have you ever been to MaggieMoo's?"

"I've never even heard of it."

"It's right there."

She pointed toward an ice cream parlor in the building to their left. On the sign above the door, a cartoon cow with long feminine eyelashes and pink lips gazed across the parking lot from within a bright pink frame. In the building opposite, a black and white awning covered the entrance of Saul Good Restaurant & Pub.

"Bovine in Pink." Jack chuckled. "I'm not sure I would have figured that one out on my own. The clue-writer must be an ice cream fan."

He found an empty parking space near the restaurant and shut off the engine.

Susanna stared at the entrance, nerves twitching. "It's such a public place. What if someone else came across the token and took it?"

"Let's don't worry about *what if.*" He pulled the keys from the ignition and reached for the door handle. "We'll do everything we can and trust God to work out the rest."

After he closed the driver's door, Susanna sat for a moment in the silent truck cab. Trust God? That was the one thing she could not do. God had let her down in the past. She couldn't risk entrusting Lizzie to Him.

THIRTEEN

Inside the restaurant, a half-dozen or so people stood in line waiting for a table. The voices of diners in the open room, combined with the rattle of dishes from the serving area along the back wall, were magnified by wood floors. Jack stood just inside the door for a moment, letting his eyes adjust to the indoor lighting and studying the room. A long bar stretched the length of the wall to his right, separated from the diners by a partition.

The first things that drew his attention were the ornate chandeliers suspended from the ceiling. Light twinkled and danced in tear-shaped droplets of crystal and amber-colored glass. *Amid Glass and Amber.* Obviously, they'd found the hiding place, but how in the world did someone hide a token in a chandelier in a public restaurant? And how were he and Susanna going to get up there to retrieve it?

He caught Susanna's eye and nodded toward the closest one. Her eyes widened as she studied it, then moved as she noted the location of each one. The paper with the second set of clues crinkled as her fingers tightened.

"Which one?" If she hadn't been standing close, he wouldn't have heard her whisper over the noise in the busy restaurant.

"Good question," Jack answered.

He examined the three chandeliers in the main room. The clue-writer who pinpointed the location of token number one with the word *Abaft* would surely be specific about which chandelier to search.

Two couples in front of him added their names to the list and stepped away from the hostess stand to wait for their table. Jack approached the girl.

"We have two. The name's Townsend."

"It'll be just a few minutes," she told him as she wrote his name on the list.

Susanna plucked at his sleeve as he moved aside. "We don't have time to eat."

"We can't just stand here and gawk. At least if we're sitting down we can get a closer look at one of them." He picked up a menu from a stack on the hostess stand and handed it to her. "Here. See if you can find a reference to the other clues in there."

While she studied the menu, his gaze slid around the room. Instead of paintings, a series of mirrors in gilded frames hung on the walls. Their surfaces reflected the twinkling light from the chandeliers. Another clue explained, *Glowing Reflection*. But which one? There were multiple mirrors from which he could see the reflection of a chandelier.

Susanna thrust the menu in front of him. "Here's a clue. This talks about the history of the restaurant, how a man named Saul Good traveled around the world collecting his favorite recipes while he was buying jewels for his father, a jeweler. Jewels are treasure, so he was a *Treasure Hunter*. And look here." She opened to the list of offerings and tapped an entry with a finger. "They're famous for their signature chocolate bar."

"That's what *Signed in Chocolate* means." Jack's gaze returned to the chandeliers. "But those just verify this restaurant as the location. Something's got to get us closer to the exact hiding place."

Susanna rubbed her fingers together, a look of distaste on her face. "Yuck. There's something sticky on the menu. I'm going to wash my hands."

"All right."

She handed Jack the paper with the clues, deposited the sticky menu on the hostess stand and disappeared down the hallway that led to the restrooms. Jack read over the list of clues again. There had to be something there, something specific. He felt certain of the reason for all the clues except the one about the glowing reflection.

The hostess seated the two couples who were ahead of him on the list. The line continued to form behind him, so the small waiting area became crowded. He glanced at his watch. Twelve-thirty. Lunchtime.

A few minutes later he caught sight of a flash of blond hair as Susanna made her way toward him. She twisted through the people standing in front of the hostess stand and stood close enough that he got a whiff of the clean lilac scent of her hair.

She leaned close. "Go to the men's room."

Had she found something? "What's in the men's room?"

Her excited whisper tickled his ear. "If it's like the ladies' room, there's one of these chandeliers hanging above the sink, right in front of a mirror." She drew back to give him a meaningful look. "The base unscrews."

That had to be it. Jack pushed through the crowd of waiting guests and made his way to the men's restroom. The moment he stepped through the door, his eyes were drawn to the chandelier where Susanna said it would be, suspended above the wash basin. It was a smaller version of the ones in the dining room, but otherwise exactly the same.

Candle-shaped bulbs reflected in the surface of a mirror mounted on the wall over the sink. Glass teardrops dangled from a decorative metal frame, some clear, some colored a dark golden amber. The center of the frame formed a rounded canister.

At least this one was within easy reach. No need to climb to reach it. Jack glanced around the room. He was alone. If someone came in, he could come up with a semi-plausible excuse for taking the thing apart.

The glass dangles clinked together when he grabbed the base. Susanna said it unscrewed, and he discovered that the bottom section was a separate piece from the rest, like a lid on an inverted jar.

"Suspended *amid glass and amber*," he whispered as he twisted.

Inside the lid, he found more duct tape. And beneath it…

Nothing.

The tape had been pried loose at one end, but there was no drawstring pouch beneath it. Jack ripped the gray tape off the metal lid and inspected it under the light. The sticky side showed evidence that something had been secured there, because the glue was slightly diminished in an area the shape of one of those canvas pouches. That meant the token had been here at one time. Since the kidnapper didn't mention number two as one of the clues to ignore, apparently he didn't have it.

So who did?

Back in the truck, Susanna pressed a fist against her stomach in a vain attempt to calm the roiling nausea. "What will he do to Lizzie if we don't have all the tokens?"

A shadow of desperation flooded her mind with images that she didn't want to see. Shutting her eyes did no good; the images remained.

"It was here." Jack fingered the patch of gray tape as he sat behind the wheel. "Someone got to it first. If it wasn't the kidnapper, then that means someone else is looking for these tokens, too."

"Then we have to hurry." She snatched up the papers and read the third set of clues aloud. *"G.C. Project. Perfect Time. Rear View of Justice. 1961. The Y at 5."*

The words might as well have been written in Latin. They brought nothing to mind at all.

"The Y at 5." Jack's gaze unfocused as he considered. "I wonder what's going on at the YMCA at five o'clock."

"Which one? There are several YMCAs around town."

By the time they found the right place, someone else might have gotten there first. What was happening with Lizzie right now? Was she frightened? Hungry? Crying for her Susu? With an effort, Susanna forced her mind away from those thoughts and focused instead on the bewildering words.

"I'm going to try my father again." Jack's fingertip tapped on the screen of his phone. "Whatever he knows about these tokens, we need to know it, too."

Susanna watched his face while he held the phone to his ear. After a moment, he shook his head. She wilted against the seat back. If Mr. Townsend held the key to getting Lizzie back, she would cry, beg and plead to get the information out of him. If that failed, she'd throttle him until he told her what he knew. But first they had to find him.

Maybe Jack's father had token number two. She clung

to the idea as if it was a lifeline. If he did, then surely he would give it up in order to get Lizzie back.

But what if he didn't have it? Who knew about the tokens besides Jack's father? Mr. Ingram had certainly known, had recovered two of them. The kidnapper knew. And the person who hid the tokens not only knew about them, but knew the location of every one. Surely there had been some communication between these men, something besides these cryptic clues.

She closed her eyes as Jack left another message for his father. Had Mr. Ingram received any calls or emails over the past week that had struck her as odd? Nothing came to mind, except—

Her eyes flew open. "Justin."

Jack gave her his full attention. "Who's Justin?"

"A guy who works in the computer department at Ingram Industries. He came by yesterday asking if Mr. Ingram had left him anything." Excitement mounted as she remembered the odd request. "I assumed he was talking about a project they'd been working on, but that was before the envelope arrived. Do you think he might have been looking for these clues and tokens?" She held up the package.

"It's worth a shot. Would he be at the office?"

She shook her head. "I doubt it. Not many people come in on Saturdays, and the computer guys work from home a lot anyway."

He turned on his phone with a tap. "What's his last name?"

Susanna closed her eyes and brought up a mental picture of the company's organizational chart, which she'd just updated the previous week. The last names of all the salaried employees scrolled through her mind. She could see the box that represented Justin's position, and his name was...

"Dickson."

She spelled the name for Jack as he keyed the letters into his touch screen.

"There's a phone listing for Justin Dickson on Chenault Road. That's not far from your office." He turned the key in the ignition and put the car in Reverse.

"Can't we just call him?" Susanna asked.

The truck rolled backward out of the parking place. He kept his eyes fixed on the rearview mirror as he answered. "A phone call might spook him."

The meaning of his words struck her with force. "Do you think he might have Lizzie?" She hadn't considered that possibility.

Jack didn't answer at first. After a pause, he lifted a shoulder. "If he does, we'll get her back."

She pictured the awkward computer programmer, with his bobbing head and questionlike stammers. He didn't strike her as the kind of person to kidnap a child. But would she recognize a kidnapper?

"If he doesn't have Lizzie," Jack continued, "then maybe he can tell us something that will help. Either way, I want to watch his face when he answers our questions."

Gratitude welled up inside her. What would she do without him? She'd be a basket case, paralyzed by fear and unable to make heads or tails out of those horrible clues. Without Jack, Lizzie would be lost to her.

An evil voice whispered inside her head. *What if the kidnapper kills her anyway?*

With an effort, she pushed the thought away and ignored the panic that hovered just beneath it, threatening to rise up and choke her in an instant. She couldn't think that way. They'd solve the clues, find the tokens. Or they'd find someone who knew something to help them, like Jack's father. And Lizzie would come home again. There *would* be a happy ending to this story.

She clutched the seat belt and refused to think about the fact that, up until now, none of her endings had ever been happy.

FOURTEEN

Justin Dickson lived on one side of a duplex midway down a neighborhood street lined with cars. Jack parked behind a Toyota in the driveway.

"Is that his car?" he asked Susanna.

Her shoulders lifted. "I have no idea. I barely know Justin."

The blinds in the front window opened. An indistinct figure inside peered through. "Well, somebody's here, anyway."

He got out of the truck and waited for Susanna to join him before approaching the porch. The door opened before he knocked. The young man who stood inside wore a wrinkled T-shirt and sweatpants. Wary but intelligent eyes acknowledged Jack's presence, then fixed on Susanna.

"Hello, Justin." Considering the stress he knew she was under, Jack marveled that she managed to speak calmly. "This is my friend, Jack Townsend. May we come in?"

The young man appeared cautious, but not, Jack realized, secretive.

Justin ran a hand across military-short hair before stepping back. "Yeah, sure. I would have cleaned up if I'd known you were coming?" The statement sounded like a question.

Jack followed Susanna into a room that appeared even smaller than it really was because of the computer equipment piled on every surface. One cushion of a plain brown couch was partially clear, but the rest bore a collection of monitors and a tangle of cords. A folding card table situated against the far wall held the corpse of a computer on its surface. The guts were spread all around, an assortment of electronic boards with switches and jumpers that looked like something out of *Star Trek*.

Justin followed his gaze. "I'm working on a buddy's computer for him? He's having a memory problem?"

The kitchen lay through an open doorway. Jack walked into the room on the pretense of looking at the contents of the card table, and took the opportunity to glance into the kitchen. Deserted. Just a few steps away, down a short hallway, the doors to a bedroom and a bathroom stood open. Not a sound came from that direction. In the compact layout of this small duplex, there were very few places to hide a kidnapped child. He exchanged a glance with Susanna, and shook his head.

Her mouth trembled for a moment, but then her shoulders straightened. "Justin, yesterday you came to my office to see if Mr. Ingram had left anything for you. What were you looking for?"

The young man's slender frame stiffened. Blood suffused his face. His mouth gaped open, and his Adam's apple bobbed up and down on his throat, but no sound emerged.

Susanna took a step toward him. "Please, Justin. It's very important."

Jack studied the young man's reaction. His eyes darted around the room, anywhere but directly at Susanna. He looked guilty, yes, but not criminally so. More like a boy caught snitching cookies.

"I—" He stopped. Gulped. "I promised not to talk about it."

"Promised who?" Jack's voice came out hard.

Justin's head jerked toward him. "Mr. Ingram. He made me swear not to tell anyone."

"Mr. Ingram is dead." Susanna's statement sounded flat, harsh, and made Justin wince. "And another life is in danger. Please, Justin. Tell us what you were looking for."

The young man's gaze bounced between Jack's face and Susanna's, his chest rising and falling with rapid breath. Finally, his head drooped forward.

"I was looking for a check?"

Not the answer Jack was expecting. "A check? What for?"

"Mr. Ingram asked me to solve a riddle for him, and if I was right, he was going to pay me a thousand bucks?"

A riddle. No doubt what that riddle was about. "You told him the answer was a 1980 Corvette being auctioned on Thursday in Louisville." Jack didn't bother to pose the statement as a question.

Justin turned a surprised look on him. "That's right. How did you know?"

Jack glanced at Susanna, and she pulled the envelope out of her purse. She flipped through the papers and extracted one.

"Is this the riddle you solved?"

Justin glanced at the page and nodded. "That wasn't the first, either. I solved two others correctly."

Jack extended his palm, and Susanna gave him the envelope. He pulled out the papers and handed them to Justin. "Are these the riddles?"

He nodded. "Yeah, there were ten of them."

At least we know there are only ten. We have them all.

"Which ones did you solve?" Jack already guessed the answer, but they had to ask.

Justin spoke as he glanced quickly at each page. "Number four was a dry cleaner's out on Todd's Road." He handed the fourth page back to Jack. "Number seven was a grandfather clock out at the Henry Clay Estate." He shook his head over page five. "I was pretty sure number five was at the Cincinnati Airport, but Mr. Ingram said he had checked it out and that must have been wrong."

Jack looked at Susanna. "He must have gone looking for the token, but it had already been recovered."

She nodded, but the young man looked confused. "I don't know anything about tokens. I just solved the riddles, and Mr. Ingram gave me a thousand bucks for each one I got right."

So, Ingram didn't tell him what was really going on. He simply used a smart kid in his company to work out the clues for him.

The longer they spent talking to Justin, the more sure Jack became that this young man wasn't involved in any illegal activity. He'd been recruited by the president of his company for a project, and he had jumped at the chance to make a few extra bucks.

Had he solved any of the others, the ones Jack and Susanna still had to recover?

"What about number three?" Jack pointed toward the papers Justin still held. "Any ideas about that one?"

His expression cleared. "Actually, yeah. I've been think-ing about it a lot." He ducked his head to hide a sheepish grin. "They eat at you, you know? Like trying to get to the next level on a game. You can't stop until you master it?"

Oh, yeah. I can relate.

Justin shoved the pile of electronic gadgets aside to clear a place on the card table and laid the papers down. Jack joined him to bend over page number three.

"The other riddles worked out to be somewhere around Lexington, so I figured whoever wrote them was sticking close to this city."

Jack grinned at him. The kid had been analyzing the clue-writer's thought process, just like him. "That's part of his pattern."

"Exactly. But I was wrong." As he gained confidence in his topic, Justin no longer posed every statement as a question. "The Cincinnati Airport isn't in the Lexington area, and neither was that auction."

Jack's mind connected the dots. "But the Cincinnati airport is actually located in northern Kentucky. And the auction was held in Louisville. So the common factor isn't the city, it's the state."

Justin nodded. "That's what I came up with. Then it was a simple matter of searching the internet to solve riddle number three. Of course the search engines match exact words, and some of these phrases aren't on a website anywhere. I had to play around with them a bit to come up with the right combination." His finger stabbed at the paper. "When I entered *1961* and *Kentucky* and *Perfect Time,* I got a hit."

Susanna stepped to Jack's side, so close he felt her arm tremble. "Where? Where is number three?"

Justin straightened. "I think it's the Floral Clock in Frankfort. The website I found says the clock is in a planter that weighs a hundred tons. It was dedicated in 1961, it has a self-adjusting mechanism so it keeps perfect time, and it was a Garden Club project."

"G.C. Project," Jack read the first clue from the page.

"The picture on the internet solved *The Y at 5*. Instead of numbers, the face of the clock spells out the word *Kentucky*. The Y is at the five-o'clock position." Justin tapped his lips with a finger. "I still don't know what *Rear View of Justice* means, though."

They fell silent. Jack thought back a few years, when he was in high school and his class visited the Kentucky State Capitol. They'd received a tour of the grounds including the Floral Clock, a gigantic timepiece mounted over a fish pond with fountains. The hands of the clock stretched over thousands of flowering plants that made up the clock face. The class had walked from there around to the front of—

He straightened. "That's it. The Floral Clock is located behind the capitol building, where the state supreme court meets."

"It has a *Rear View of Justice*." Susanna folded her arms with an irritated jerk. "Why couldn't he have said it was abaft? We would have known what that meant immediately."

Jack glanced at his watch. One-thirty. The drive to Frankfort would take half an hour each way, so they wouldn't lose too much time picking up token number three, provided it hadn't been retrieved by someone else. But there were still two clues to solve. Might as well take advantage of Justin's sharp mind while they could.

He sifted through the papers until he found pages six and ten. "Have you come up with anything for these?"

The first part of the ride to Frankfort was spent in silence while Susanna battled her thoughts. Soft music came from speakers in the truck's dashboard, but if Jack had turned it on to distract her, his plan failed. If she kept thinking about the terrible things that might happen to Lizzie, she would lose her mind.

She pulled the four tokens out of the cardboard envelope and clutched them in a fist. The kidnapper expected eight. If all went well, they'd get the one hidden in the Floral Clock in Frankfort, and then recover the last two, though Jack and Justin weren't confident about the location of number ten.

She dropped the tokens back in the envelope, laid it across her lap and twisted beneath the seat belt so she sat facing Jack. "Listening to you and Justin work out those clues was amazing."

"He's a smart guy. Ingram knew what he was doing when he recruited him to help."

"You're both smart." Gratitude welled up so suddenly it threatened to choke her. "I can't thank you enough for helping us."

"I'm glad you called me."

"I had no choice." Her gaze dropped to her clasped hands resting in her lap. "I have no one else."

"That's not true," he said. "You always have God."

His words, though spoken lightly, turned the air between them to lead. A bitter reply shot out of Susanna's mouth before she could stop it. "God's never been here for me before. I certainly don't expect Him to start now."

From the corner of her eye, she saw Jack's head jerk sideways. "Why would you say that?"

"Because it's true. Where was God when my fiancé was attacking my little sister? Where was He when my family's house burned down? Or in the days that followed, when Marti and Mom lay in the hospital, suffering?" Though embarrassed at the bitterness in her voice, Susanna couldn't stop the flood of words. "I prayed constantly for them. But either He didn't hear my prayers, or He decided to take an innocent baby's mother and grandmother and grandfather all at once."

"He saved Lizzie." Jack spoke quietly. "And her aunt."

"It isn't enough." She forced herself to draw in a full, deep breath in an effort to calm down. "Prayer is a waste of breath."

In the silence that followed, shame for her harsh words sent heat into Susanna's face. What kind of ungrateful heathen must Jack think her?

When Jack finally spoke, he sounded thoughtful. "I understand why you'd feel that way. Smarter people than me have tried to answer the question of why God answers some prayers but seems to ignore others." He shook his head. "One thing I do know, though. Just because we don't see Him answer the way we want all the time, that doesn't mean we should stop asking."

Tears prickled behind her eyes. *I can't handle being ignored again. Not about this. Not when Lizzie's life is at stake.*

She schooled her voice to a light reply. "How about if I leave the praying to you? You seem to have more experience at it than me."

"All right."

He fell silent. As his pause stretched longer and longer, Susanna risked a glance at him. His lips moved almost imperceptibly, but no sound came out.

He's praying right now.

The realization hit her with something like shock. Jack really was praying for Lizzie. Even more shocking was an accompanying sense of reassurance.

FIFTEEN

The dome of the Kentucky state capitol building rose above a columned entrance beyond a wide stone stairway. More snow covered the ground here than at home in Lexington, less than thirty miles away. The decorative median that divided the long avenue leading to the capitol wore a blanket of white. Susanna peered through the windshield as Jack guided the truck around the side of the building, past a nearly deserted parking lot.

"There it is." She stabbed at the glass with a finger.

A thin layer of snow covered the gigantic stone circle mounted at an angle over a walled fountain. Icicles dripped from the lowest point, beneath the six-o'clock position. The long blue beams that formed the clock's hands indicated the time as two-twenty, though the snow was deep enough to hide the letters on the face.

Susanna's gaze was drawn to a dark figure huddled in the midst of the snow. "Is someone doing maintenance on it?"

As she voiced the question, she realized the man was stooped over the five-o'clock position. That was no maintenance man. They'd come upon someone else searching for token number three. Her pulse accelerated at the same moment Jack's foot stomped on the gas pedal.

The truck zoomed across the short distance and screeched to a halt in front of the stairs leading up to the clock. Before Jack could shove the gearshift lever into Park she was out of the truck and dashing up the stairs.

"Susanna, wait!"

The man on the clock face looked up, then returned to his task, brushing the snow away with hurried gestures.

She ignored Jack's shout. They *had* to get that token for Lizzie's sake. Footsteps behind her gave evidence that Jack was fast on her heels as she raced to the wall surrounding the pond. The low end of the clock loomed above her, too far away to jump. How had that man gotten up there? She took in the layout in a second. The stone wall didn't completely encircle the giant clock, but stopped halfway around to connect to each side of the base. He must have climbed from there.

Jack apparently reached the same conclusion. Before she could move, he dashed around the walkway and leaped onto the wall. He grabbed the concrete edge of the clock, and pulled himself up as if it were a chin-up bar at the gym.

The man on the clock leaned backward on his haunches, surprise etched on his clean-shaven features. A stab of dismay struck Susanna when she saw a familiar-looking string dangling from his fist. The drawstring from the bags that held the tokens.

They'd failed.

"Oh, please." She didn't even try to stop the sob that welled up in her chest. "We need that token. It's a matter of life and death."

The man's glance rested on her for only a moment, then returned to Jack. Questions flooded his face.

"Jack?"

Susanna could only see the back of Jack's head, but she heard the confusion in his voice. "Preston?"

Surprise dried her tears. Jack knew this guy?

Jack hopped off the wall and backed up as the man climbed down. He brushed dirt from a brown suede jacket. Wet spots darkened his slacks at the knees where he'd knelt in the snow, looking for the token.

When he stood on the walkway beside them, he peered into Jack's face. "What are you doing here, Jack?"

"Apparently the same thing you're doing." Jack jerked his head in the direction of the object in the man's hand. "We came to get that."

"This?" There was no mistaking the surprise in his voice. He opened his hand to reveal the drawstring pouch. The eyes he raised held the glitter of triumph. "Your father told you about the Game. That means he's disqualified himself."

Jack's mouth fell open, but no words came.

The sight of the small bag in the man's palm stirred the barely controlled panic inside Susanna. She placed her folded hands beneath her chin and let him see the desperation in her face. "Please let us have it."

The man's fingers closed around the token. "I'm sorry. Have we met?"

Jack gestured as he made the introduction. "Susanna Trent, this is Preston Phillips."

She peered more closely. Preston Phillips's name was well-known around the state. He'd made his fortune breeding and training thoroughbreds, a highly regarded profession in the Bluegrass state. Of course he and Jack would be acquainted. Wealthy men all knew each other, didn't they?

Preston extended his hand, and Susanna took it automatically. His skin was cold and damp from digging in the snow.

"Susanna worked for Tom Ingram," Jack finished.

The icy fingers tightened on her hand.

"A tragedy." He shook his head. "Tom was a fine man. He'll be missed."

"Yes, he will." Her reply came automatically. She could not tear her gaze from the drawstring pouch. "Mr. Phillips, what do you mean Mr. Townsend disqualified himself? What game are you talking about?"

He shoved the pouch into the pocket of his slacks. "Sorry. I'm not going to break the rules. I can't say a word."

When he started to back away, Susanna rushed forward and grabbed his arm. "You don't understand. A little girl has been kidnapped. We need that token to get her back."

There was no mistaking the confusion on the man's face. He raised his head to look from her to Jack. "What is she talking about?"

Jack raised his eyebrows, asking a silent question of her. Should they confide in this man? Would that endanger Lizzie? On the other hand, what choice did they have? Preston obviously knew the reason behind the clues and tokens. She gave her permission to Jack with a nod.

During his brief recounting of the past two days, Susanna watched Preston's face. The man's eyes widened and his jaw went slack. When Jack reached the part about the kidnapper's phone call, he interrupted.

"You have to get the police involved." The authority with which he spoke bore evidence to the fact that he was accustomed to being obeyed.

"We can't," Susanna insisted. "He said he'll kill her."

"Of course he's going to say that. He'd much rather

deal with a terrified and compliant woman than trained professionals."

She set her jaw, prepared to argue the point, but Jack stopped her with a hand on her arm.

"Preston, now that you know how serious our situation is, will you tell us what's going on? What is this game you mentioned?"

He half turned away to look out over the parking lot. "I'd rather you ask your father."

"I tried last night," Jack said. "He wouldn't tell me anything. And today I haven't been able to get in touch with him."

For a long moment, she thought Preston wouldn't answer. The deep creases in his high forehead moved and changed, alive with his thoughts. When he reached a decision, the lines cleared.

Thank goodness. Now they would finally get some real answers.

"It started with a poker game. A group of us get together at the club every month and play."

Mr. Ingram had talked about his monthly poker game. The stakes were kept high in order to keep the game exclusive. Only the wealthiest in Lexington were invited to play. He'd joked about robbing from the rich to give to the rich, not having any idea how repugnant that idea was to Susanna. He had instructed her to keep that evening clear on his schedule every month.

"A couple months ago some of us suggested an idea to up the ante a bit. We decided to create a different kind of game, one that would require some knowledge. You know." His gaze bounced between the two of them. "An intelligence game instead of a game of chance. Just for fun. Nothing serious."

He shoved his hands in the pockets of his pants. Susanna

realized she could hardly feel her feet anymore, so cold were they from standing on the frozen walkway. She wrapped her arms around her middle.

Jack was so intent on Preston's face he seemed not to notice the cold. "You came up with clues that would test your knowledge of places around Kentucky."

"Well, *we* didn't. We appointed a Game Master to do that, and to hide the tokens. We each chipped in some money."

"How much?" Susanna asked.

He lifted a shoulder. "Just a hundred thousand each."

Just a hundred thousand? Outraged, her spine stiffened. A bunch of rich men playing with money as if it came from a Monopoly game. Didn't they realize what a hundred thousand dollars would mean to underprivileged people?

"And how many people are playing this game?" Jack asked.

"Ten."

"That's a million dollars." She didn't bother filtering out the shock of the look she turned on Jack.

"A lot of money." His mouth went hard. "Enough to kill for. And to kidnap for."

Preston's head jerked upward. "That's ridiculous. No one murdered Ingram for three tokens. These are wealthy men. The money isn't the point of the Game. We're in it for the fun, the bragging rights."

"Apparently someone *is* in it for the money," Susanna snapped. "One of you strangled Mr. Ingram and kidnapped my niece."

"Impossible." The man's face became stubborn.

Jack interrupted before she could respond to his infuriating insistence. "So you each received the ten clues and you've all been trying to solve them and retrieve the tokens."

"That's right." He patted his pocket. "This is the first one I've managed to find, though. I had one figured out, but someone got to the dry cleaner's before me."

Something still didn't make sense to Susanna. "This game isn't illegal, is it? The kidnapper told me that Mr. Ingram was involved in illegal activity."

Preston didn't meet either of their gazes. "Well, this kind of gambling isn't exactly condoned by the gaming commission. Especially since the money is on deposit in an offshore account. It's up to the winner to decide whether or not to pay the taxes. But I think it's safe to say the kidnapper exaggerated the situation to force your cooperation."

"I can't believe my father would get involved in this game." Jack shook his head. "It doesn't seem like something he'd agree to."

A humorless blast of laughter erupted from Preston. "You don't know your father, then. The Game was R.H.'s idea to begin with."

A chill that had nothing to do with the frigid air crept over Susanna. She stole a look at Jack. He'd been unable to reach his father all day, ever since Lizzie disappeared. Her stomach gave a nauseous twist. Could Jack's father have taken Lizzie?

Jack couldn't meet Susanna's gaze. His thoughts reeled with the idea of his father, R. H. Townsend, coming up with this scheme. He couldn't believe it. Sure, R.H. would drop a bundle at the races, or in a poker game. But a hundred thousand dollars on a scavenger hunt for a bunch of worthless pieces of metal? It was beyond comprehension. Especially since R.H.'s knowledge was limited to business matters, not the sights around the Bluegrass state. His company had been his focus for so long that Jack doubted if he'd ever visited the Kentucky Horse Park or the Floral Clock.

But someone had been killed, and a child had been kidnapped. And the clues all pointed toward Jack's father.

"Hang on a second," he told Susanna and Preston.

He slid the phone out of his pocket and dialed R.H.'s office number. The line rang, and then was answered by the company's voice mail system. He tried the home number and even his father's cell phone. No answer on any of them.

Jack hung up and dialed another number. Richard, the chief of staff, was in the office whenever R.H. was there. Maybe he'd know how to get hold of his boss.

Richard's phone went to voice mail, too.

Desperation made his muscles tight, his motions jerky, as he slid his finger across the phone's screen. His phone's contact list was synced with the office directory, including the private address book for the executive's personal contact numbers. He found the entry for Alice Lester, his father's administrative assistant, and tapped the screen to dial.

Alice answered on the third ring. "Hello?"

"Alice, it's Jack." By exercising rigid control, he filtered most of the tension out of his voice. "I've been trying to reach my father all day. He's not at home or the office, and he's not answering his cell phone. You don't know where he is, do you?"

He was aware of Susanna and Preston standing behind him. His heart beat five times before Alice answered.

"He told me that he'd be out of touch today, Jack. You know he rarely turns on his cell phone."

"Where is he?" He winced at the unintended volume.

Another long pause. "He didn't say. Is something wrong?"

The muscles in Jack's neck were so tight they felt as though they might cut off his windpipe. Where would R.H. go that he wouldn't tell his longtime assistant?

"Alice, if you happen to hear from him, please tell him to call me. It's important."

"Why would I hear from him on a Saturday, Jack?"

Her voice sounded odd, her suspicions fully aroused.

"Never mind. Goodbye, Alice." He disconnected the call before she could ask any more questions.

He pocketed the phone and told Susanna and Preston, "He's out of touch somewhere. His administrative assistant doesn't know where."

He couldn't bring himself to look at Susanna. Though he could not believe that his father would purposefully harm a child, there seemed little doubt that R.H. was responsible for Lizzie's kidnapping. At least inadvertently, by inventing this crazy scheme, if not more directly.

R.H., where are you?

Another possibility whispered an ugly suspicion in Jack's ear.

What if he suffered the same fate as Tom Ingram?

No. They might not always get along, but Jack couldn't bear the image of his father's strangled body.

Lord, don't let him be dead.

"This has gone on long enough." Preston dug the token out of his pocket and held it in a clenched fist. "This is not worth anyone's life, especially an innocent child's. It's time to contact the police."

"I can't." Tears glittered in Susanna's eyes. "I have to follow the kidnapper's instructions. Please, will you just give me that token?"

Me, she said. Not *us*. And invisible fist grabbed Jack's stomach and squeezed. *She blames me for my father's actions.*

Jack squared his shoulders. If that was the way it had to be, he'd bear it. But he had to convince her of the truth of Preston's words. The situation had moved beyond their abilities.

"Susanna, listen to me." He grabbed her by the arms and forced her to face him. "Preston's right. Even with this token, we don't have them all. There's no guarantee the kidnapper will return Lizzie. We need to turn this over to the professionals." He ignored Preston and lowered his voice. "Not all police officers are like the one you talked to in Tennessee."

Tortured eyes held his for a long moment. Then she stepped forward and wrapped her arms around him. Her face pressed against his shoulder while deep, shuddering cries racked her body. Jack pressed her close to him. Maybe she didn't blame him after all. Maybe she even trusted him. He formed a wordless prayer of thanks. With every tear she shed, his determination to find Lizzie grew. Then he could wipe those tears away. But he was out of ideas. The best way, the only way, was to let the police do their jobs.

"Okay." The words were muffled by his jacket. "Call Detective Rollins."

Thank You, Lord.

"Good. We'll take him the clues and the tokens we've managed to recover." He gave Preston a meaningful stare.

The man's shoulders heaved. "He'll probably want this one, too."

"And a list of names," Jack told him.

Preston's snort held a touch of resignation. "You might as well have the detective meet us at the home of Lawrence Van Cleve."

Susanna turned in Jack's arms. "Who?"

His smile turned grim. "Judge Lawrence Van Cleve. He's the Game Master."

Stunned, Jack could only stare at the man's face. The Game Master, the writer of the clues, was a *judge?*

SIXTEEN

Judge Lawrence Van Cleve's driveway curved away from the road across a sprawling lawn to a stately antebellum home. Susanna watched Preston's Expedition through the windshield of Jack's truck. It rolled to a stop on the circular blacktop in front of a paved walkway leading to the front door.

Jack parked a few feet behind, and glanced in the rearview mirror. "They're here."

Susanna turned in her seat in time to see a plain white Ford make the turn from the road, followed by two police cruisers. Through the Ford's window she glimpsed the familiar face of Detective Rollins.

During the drive from Frankfort, she'd made the phone call while Jack drove. They'd decided the best course of action was to reveal as little information as possible over the phone, so she merely told him that they had uncovered some important information in the murder case, and that urgent action was required to prevent another death. Rollins's voice had grown taciturn during the brief conversation, especially when she asked him to meet them at Judge Van Cleve's residence.

"I'll be there in fifteen minutes," he had snapped, and disconnected the call.

As she climbed out of the truck, Susanna felt like a wayward child heading into her father's study to be scolded. Without a doubt, Rollins would berate her for not reporting the kidnapping immediately.

She rounded the bumper and stood close to Jack. He wrapped an arm around her shoulders, and she leaned into him, drawing courage from his strength. What would she have done without him today? Since the moment her world had blown apart, he'd provided the only hope she could grasp on to. What an odd twist that she, who had been burned in the worst way possible by a rich man's son, would come to trust in another rich man's son.

And she did trust Jack. His father, however, was cut from the same cloth as Bruce. If it turned out he was responsible for this kidnapping and Mr. Ingram's murder, she wouldn't rest until she saw him rotting in prison.

Rollins approached, his expression grim. "Ms. Trent, would you care to enlighten me about this urgent matter you mentioned on the phone?"

She opened her mouth to blurt out an answer when the door to the house opened. An elderly gentleman with a full head of thick, white hair and piercing eyes stepped outside. Though she had never met Judge Van Cleve, he bore the unmistakable carriage of authority that identified him.

"You've arrived at once. How fortuitous. Now we can all hear the explanations together." His gesture invited them inside. "Please."

"Explanations would be good," Rollins growled as he brushed past Susanna and Jack.

Preston joined them on the sidewalk. "I called on the way to let the judge know we were coming. Figured that was better than blindsiding him."

Susanna nodded as, at the doorway, both Jack and Preston paused to allow her to enter first. She stepped into an elaborately decorated hallway. Dark hardwood gleamed beneath her feet and from a curved banister leading to a wide landing. A high ceiling towered above, giving the place the hollow feel of a cathedral.

When the two uniformed police officers entered, Judge Van Cleve closed the door and turned toward them. "Let's go into the study." He awarded Susanna a kind smile. "This way, my dear."

She followed him down the hallway and through a doorway on the left. Thick carpet cushioned her step when she entered. Floor-to-ceiling bookcases lined the walls on either side, the shelves completely full of books. An ornate desk sat in front of wide French doors, two dark red leather armchairs facing it. A matching sofa stood against the remaining wall. The lingering scent of pipe tobacco mingled with the odor of old books.

The judge scooted a chair around so it faced the room and gestured to Susanna. "Please sit here." He circled the desk toward his own chair, leaving the men to sort out their own seating arrangements.

Susanna placed her purse on the floor beside the chair and slid onto the soft leather. Jack stood beside her while Preston took the other armchair. After a curt nod toward the two officers, who took up stances near the door, Rollins sat in the center of the couch.

"Would someone please explain what this is all about?" The glare the detective aimed at Susanna and Jack softened into a glance of respect when he turned it on Judge Van Cleve. "I was told new evidence has arisen regarding a murder case."

"Ah, yes. Tom Ingram." The judge leaned back in his chair, hands folded across his middle. "Quite disturbing." He shifted his gaze to Susanna. "Would you care to explain, my dear?"

All eyes turned toward her. Susanna felt the weight of them, especially Detective Rollins's. She ignored him and focused her attention on the fatherly figure of Judge Van Cleve.

"It all started last Thursday when Mr. Ingram sent me to an auction in Louisville to buy a Corvette."

She related the facts as she and Jack had discovered them, hesitantly at first but then with more confidence. When she described the initial phone call from the killer, she risked a glance at Rollins's face. His lips formed a rigid white line. She shuddered and did not look at him again. Tears almost overtook her when she told them about coming out of the bathroom to find the back window open and Lizzie gone. Jack placed a hand on her shoulder and squeezed. She drew comfort from the contact, took a deep breath and continued, bringing them all up to the moment they'd arrived here.

Rollins waited until she stopped before exploding. "You withheld evidence in a murder investigation!" He leaped off the couch and paced to the center of the room. "I could arrest you for that alone. Not to mention the fact that you failed to report a kidnapping." A purple vein throbbed in his forehead. "If you'd called us immediately, we could have had an Amber Alert out in minutes. We would have caught this guy."

"That's exactly what I didn't want." Angry tears blurred her vision as she snatched her purse off the floor and rummaged inside it. "Look at this." She thrust the note the kidnapper had left on the bed toward him. "He said he'd hurt her if I called the police. And look here." She opened the envelope to reveal the lock of golden hair. "He really will do it if we don't give him all the tokens."

Rollins clasped his hands behind his back and jerked his head toward one of the officers, who opened a canvas bag. He pulled on a pair of rubber gloves and took the note and the envelope from Susanna.

She turned toward the judge. "Please, just tell us where the rest of the tokens are hidden. That will satisfy him, and he'll give Lizzie back."

Judge Van Cleve's eyes became heavy with sympathy. "Of course I will, but, my dear, do you really think you can bargain with a madman? He's already killed once."

Susanna dropped her head forward and covered her face with her hands.

"Maybe twice." Jack spoke from behind her. "My father is missing. Even his assistant said she doesn't know where he is. I'm afraid he's either become a victim, or…"

The misery Susanna saw in his eyes wrenched her heart. If it turned out R. H. Townsend had strangled his friend and kidnapped Lizzie, would Jack be able to handle the shame?

"That's it. One person murdered, two missing." Rollins rounded on Preston. "I want the name of everyone involved in this game."

Preston and Judge Van Cleve exchanged a guarded glance.

The judge cleared his throat. "If the press gets hold of this list, we'll be flooded with reporters within minutes. May we rely on your discretion?"

Rollins hesitated only a moment before replying. "Of course, Your Honor."

Susanna listened with growing amazement as Preston and Judge Van Cleve listed the Game players. Most of the names were recognizable, commonly mentioned in the newspaper and even profiled on television. She'd known Mr. Ingram's poker group consisted of wealthy men, but she'd only heard him mention a few. The press would, indeed, be all over this if word leaked out. And that would be bad for Lizzie.

"Who else knew about this game?" The detective addressed the judge.

"No one," Van Cleve replied with a confident nod. "The rules specifically state that a player will be disqualified if he discusses the Game with anyone else."

"Actually, there is one other person." Susanna gave him an apologetic grimace. "Mr. Ingram enlisted the help of one of his employees, Justin Dickson. We talked to him this morning."

"Address?" Rollins snapped.

Susanna didn't hesitate to give it. *I'm sorry, Justin.*

The detective pointed toward the officers, who'd been recording the names as they were given. "There's your suspect list. Round them up and bring them downtown for questioning." He turned to Jack. "Who's your father's assistant?"

Jack straightened, his surprise apparent. "Her name is Alice Lester."

"Got an address?" When Jack hesitated, Rollins snapped, "We need to verify his schedule for this weekend and for Thursday night."

Jack's face went white, but he made no argument. Susanna watched as he pulled up the address on his phone. Poor Alice Lester was about to have her weekend interrupted. But no one knew better than Susanna what close tabs an executive secretary kept on her boss. Maybe the woman would be able to give the police some information that would lead them to Mr. Townsend. And if he had Lizzie…

Oh, please help us find her!

The desperate prayer formed automatically, before she could stop it.

The officers left the room to carry out Rollins's order.

Preston stared after them, clearly disturbed. "I think you're wasting time with the Game players. There's no way any of us are involved with kidnapping and murder."

"I agree," the judge said. "The idea that any of these men would murder one of our own is ludicrous."

Yet they consider committing tax evasion, which is a felony. Susanna glanced at Jack, and knew his thoughts mirrored hers.

Rollins ignored their protest and looked at her. "I'm going to need a description of your niece, and a picture. It's been a few hours, and the longer we wait to activate the Amber Alert system—"

"No!" Susanna came out of the chair. Control of the situation, of Lizzie's fate, was slipping from her grasp with every second that passed. "If you do that, he'll hear it on the news. He'll know I went to the police." She turned an accusatory glance toward Jack. "This is exactly what I was afraid would happen."

A familiar noise interrupted her. From the depths of her purse, her cell phone rang. For a moment, no one moved. Before it began the second ring, Susanna dove for her handbag. She plunged her hand in and felt along the bottom for the vibration. Her fingers touched hard plastic, and she pulled out the phone. The number displayed on the screen was the same one from this morning. Her heart galloped like one of Preston's racehorses.

"It's him," she told the men in the room. "It's the kidnapper."

SEVENTEEN

Rollins took a step toward her and issued an urgent command. "Don't tell him that you've contacted anyone. Let him think you're alone." He gestured for the others to gather close. "When he talks, hold the phone so each can hear it. Maybe they'll recognize his voice."

The men circled her, Rollins directly in front. His intent stare never left her face.

With a finger that would not hold steady, she pressed the button to answer the call. "Hello?"

"How are you coming on those clues?" The same voice, muffled like before.

"I have five now."

Should she tell him about the one missing from the chandelier in the restaurant? No. With the Game Master's help they could retrieve the last two. Maybe seven tokens would appease him enough to arrange a transfer—Lizzie for the tokens. Then Detective Rollins could do whatever he wanted to put the kidnapper behind bars, *after* Lizzie had been safely returned.

She leaned close to the judge and tilted the phone so he could hear the reply.

"That's good. Which two did you find?"

Judge Van Cleve leaned away, shaking his head. He stepped back and Preston took his place.

"I found number one and number three."

"Good for you. I thought someone else must have beaten me to number one. I couldn't find anything on that Man O'War monument. Where was number three?"

Preston squinted his eyes shut as he listened. Then he, too, shook his head and backed away.

Rollins motioned for Jack to listen. A fearful expression crossed his features.

He's afraid he'll recognize his father's voice. A corner of her brain experienced a pang of sympathy for Jack, but she didn't have time for that right now. She had to focus on finding Lizzie.

He wiped the expression away and placed his ear close to the phone.

"It was in Frankfort, at the Floral Clock."

"Interesting."

Jack made a circular motion with his hand, a sign to encourage the kidnapper to keep talking. He needed more than one word to see if he recognized the voice.

"How is Lizzie?" The phone shook in her hand. "Is she okay?"

"You can judge for yourself."

The noise that followed sounded like something rubbing against the phone. A second later, Lizzie's familiar voice filled her ear.

"Susu, is that you? When are you coming to get me?"

Susanna's knees wobbled from relief. Jack's arm slipped around her waist, holding her up and pulling her close to his side.

She couldn't cry. That would only upset Lizzie. "Hi, sweetie. Are you okay?"

"The man's a meanie, Susu. He said I can't pet the

horsies. The TV don't get Cartoon Network, only boring stuff." She stopped, then went on grudgingly, "But I can have all the peppermint candies I want."

Susanna was still doing battle with the lump of tears that clogged her throat when more shuffling sounded on the line. The kidnapper's muffled voice returned.

"Nine o'clock tomorrow night will be here before you know it. Work faster."

"I will. I—" Susanna realized she spoke to dead air.

The effort of holding back the wave of emotion became too much. She gave in, and collapsed in tears.

Jack supported Susanna's weight over to the leather chair, and settled her in it. The judge snatched two tissues from the box on his desk and handed them to her. She buried her face in them.

Jack faced Detective Rollins. "The voice was purposefully muffled, but I'm ninety-percent sure that wasn't my father."

"I don't think so, either," Preston agreed. "R.H.'s voice is lower, almost booming. This man speaks in a higher tone."

"Voices can be disguised," Rollins said.

Jack started to argue, but closed his mouth on the words. How could he defend R.H. when the evidence against him was undeniable? He'd proposed this game. Refused to discuss it when Jack pressed him last night. His car wasn't in the garage where it should have been Thursday night, the night of Ingram's murder.

Another phone rang. The detective unclipped his cell from his belt. "Rollins." After a moment, his face took on the consistency of stone. "We'll wait here." He disconnected the call. "We may have just gotten a break."

Susanna was across the room in a flash. "You've found Lizzie?"

Unexpected compassion softened the habitual grim stare when he looked down at her. "No, I'm afraid not. But one of the officers may have a lead. He'll be here in a minute."

At the look of desperation on her face, Jack's fists tightened at his side. He hated this helpless feeling. Susanna had called him for help, had trusted him enough to place Lizzie's life in his care. What had he done so far? Managed to solve a few riddles. Big deal.

"Should we go after the other tokens?" It might not be much, but anything would be better than sitting around here. He crossed the room to Judge Van Cleve's desk. "As far as I know, numbers six and ten are still out there. I think I know where they are, but we haven't checked yet."

Preston joined him in front of the judge's desk. "Where is six? That one has been driving me crazy."

Jack watched the Game Master's face as he answered. "It's beneath Seat Number 28, Row R, Section 213 at Rupp Arena."

A smile hovered around the edges of Van Cleve's mouth. "Very good. And number ten?"

"In Room 146 at Homestead Nursing Center, in the middle dresser drawer."

"Taped to the bottom of the drawer, actually. That's my mother's room." The judge rocked backward and folded his hands across his stomach. "I thought she'd enjoy a few male visitors. She's a terrible flirt, even at ninety-seven."

"Well, I'll be." Preston gave a low whistle. "How'd you figure that out?"

Jack shrugged. "There's a pattern to the clues. The judge likes obscure facts and words, and when he uses numbers they're always directional. Once I figured that out, it wasn't too hard. Besides, I had help from a computer guru on those two."

Susanna spoke up. "Don't let him fool you. He figured out more of the clues than Justin. I was there." She addressed Detective Rollins. "Can we go get them?"

"I'll send someone." He looked as if he was going to say more, but a doorbell sounded from the hallway. "That will be Officer Parkins. If you don't mind, Your Honor, I'll let him in."

Van Cleve merely extended a hand, palm up, by way of permission. When the detective left the room, he turned a speculative stare on Jack. "You analyzed my thought processes, young man. I'm impressed."

Jack was about to reply that all his analytical skills hadn't managed to accomplish the one thing he desperately wanted, to return Lizzie to Susanna's arms, when Rollins returned to the room. The words evaporated from his mind when he caught sight of the people following the detective. Shock made him revert to the name he hadn't used in three years.

"Father!"

R.H.'s eyebrows drew together. "Jack. I thought that was your truck out front. What is the meaning of…"

His eyes swept the room, past Susanna and Preston, and came to rest on Van Cleve. "Lawrence, maybe you can explain what's going on. Why am I here?"

"It's a serious matter, R.H."

Jack barely heard the judge's answer. He'd just caught sight of the person standing behind his father.

"Alice? What are you doing here?"

Red splotches appeared on Alice's neck. "Jack, I hated to mislead you when you called. I'm sorry."

Mislead me? "I don't understand."

Rollins answered. "Apparently when Officer Parkins

arrived at Ms. Lester's home to question her about Mr. Townsend's whereabouts, he answered the door himself." The detective looked at the officer for verification.

The man nodded. "Says he's been there all day. Since last night, in fact. The lady says so, too."

The red on Alice's neck crept up into her face. R.H. seemed suddenly intent on studying the titles on the books lining the bookshelves.

"What?" Jack couldn't believe his ears. His father and *Alice?*

Susanna crossed the room to stand in front of R.H. "Mr. Townsend, please say you know where my niece is." The pleading in her voice cinched Jack's stomach tight.

Her tearful plea apparently penetrated even R.H.'s tough shell. When he spoke, his voice was softer than Jack had ever heard it. "I'm sorry. I wish I could help, but I don't know what you're talking about."

Susanna turned away, her face devoid of hope. Jack extended his arm, and she moved into his embrace.

Even Detective Rollins's voice had lost its angry edge. "Mr. Townsend, can you account for your whereabouts Thursday afternoon and evening?"

For a moment Jack thought R.H. would refuse. His chest puffed out indignantly, but after a glance at Susanna's silently weeping form, it deflated.

"I was at the office until eight-thirty. I guess the security cameras can verify that. Then I went home for a while." His gaze slid from the detective to Jack for an instant, then returned. "Then I went to Alice's house around ten."

"An odd time for a social visit." Rollins's comment was desert dry.

Alice's face turned crimson, but R.H.'s head shot up. "I had a matter I needed to discuss with her."

Jack knew the matter that drove his father out that late at night.

I was right. He was upset by his friend's death. I knew it.

As the meaning of R.H.'s action became clear, amazement stole over Jack. He'd been upset, and he'd gone to *Alice* for comfort. That meant he considered her an emotional confidante. Just how long had this relationship been going on?

So many questions made sense now. No wonder Alice stayed at Townsend Steakhouses, working for a tyrant. She loved him. Jack had only to see the look she fixed on R.H. as she nodded, verifying his story, for proof of her devotion to him.

Rollins didn't back down a single inch. "We'll need access to those security recordings from Thursday night."

"Fine." R.H. waved a hand in the air with an impatient gesture. "Would someone please tell me what's going on?"

This time the recounting of the story fell to Detective Rollins. He'd obviously been paying attention. He didn't miss a single detail.

Jack watched the reactions playing across his father's face. Shock, outrage and fury gave way to a grim mask as he considered the seriousness of the situation.

Rollins finished with the phone call from the kidnapper. "So our next step is to question everyone who knows about this game. Judge Van Cleve and Mr. Phillips have identified them all, and they're being—" his smile held no humor "—*escorted* to headquarters for questioning."

A look passed between R.H. and Alice. She nodded slightly, and R.H. heaved a sigh. "Not everyone."

Susanna stiffened beneath Jack's arm. "Who else knows?"

Behind them, Preston let out a loud exclamation. "Am I the only one who stuck to the rules and tried to solve the clues myself?"

Ingram had enlisted Justin's help. A list of people his father may have consulted ran through Jack's mind. Someone from the office, obviously, since R.H. had few acquaintances elsewhere. Did they have a whiz kid like Justin somewhere in the organization that Jack didn't know about?

R.H. blurted the name. "My chief of staff, Richard Stratton."

The moment he heard the name, Jack knew they'd just identified the kidnapper.

EIGHTEEN

The name meant nothing to Susanna, but Jack's body beside her went stiff.

"That's him." His voice held no trace of doubt. "Richard is the killer."

"Preposterous." R.H. shook his head. "He's an intelligent man, a good worker. He wouldn't hurt anyone." His gaze flickered toward Susanna for a moment, then back to Jack. "Especially a little girl."

"Do you have an address for him?" Rollins pointed toward the officer, who whipped out a pen and notepad.

"How would I know? I've never been to the man's home." R.H. seemed slightly offended at the suggestion.

Beside her, Jack pulled the phone out of his pocket once again. "I have it." His finger glided over the screen, and he read the address to the officer.

"This is a waste of time." R.H. gathered his full height and leveled a glare on Rollins. "Why don't you work on finding the little girl instead of chasing after shadows that won't amount to anything?"

Rollins opened his mouth to answer, but Jack spoke first.

"How long has Richard known about the Game?"

His father sent an uncomfortable glance toward the

judge before answering. "Since the beginning. It was his idea."

"You said it was your idea." Preston folded his arms across his chest. "Seems nothing about the Game has been on the up-and-up since the beginning."

R.H. had the grace to look embarrassed. "Of course it has. And I never actually *said* it was my idea. I merely made a suggestion. Does it matter whose idea it was? We all agreed to it. We outlined the rules." He waved a hand in the judge's direction. "Lawrence came up with the riddles, hid the tokens."

Tokens! The kidnapper had told Susanna not to waste her time trying to find numbers five and eight. Presumably, that meant he already had them. She'd forgotten to mention that when she relayed the details of that terrible phone call.

She addressed R.H. "Has this Richard found any of the tokens yet?"

He nodded. "Not as many as Jack, though. He's only found two of them."

Excitement prickled along her nerve endings. Maybe this was the proof they needed. "Which ones?"

"One up in the Cincinnati airport, and the other in Triangle Park downtown."

Jack exploded into motion. He crossed the room in two long-legged strides to stand face-to-face with Detective Rollins. "Those are the two the kidnapper told Susanna not to waste her time on. Five and eight. I'm telling you, Richard Stratton has Lizzie."

Hope soared like a balloon inside her. Maybe coming to the police hadn't been the wrong move after all.

"Let's go get her right now." She started for the door.

Rollins's voice stopped her. "Hold on a minute. We're

getting ahead of ourselves here." He looked at the officer. "Get on the radio and have someone check out Stratton's address. Quietly. If he has the girl, we don't want to spook him." The officer left the room, and the detective addressed the rest of them. "This doesn't change anything. We're still going down to headquarters to go over everything again."

"But why?" Frustration threatened to choke her. "We already know who took Lizzie."

His expression became infuriatingly patient. "Ms. Trent, we don't know anything at this point." Jack started to interrupt, but the detective held up a hand to forestall him. "I admit this lead looks promising. But suppose this Stratton does have your niece. We can't simply barge in and ask him nicely to return her, can we?"

Did he think her a simpleton? She clenched her teeth and ground out an answer. "Of course not. We need a plan."

"Precisely. Which is why I'm going to get the federal authorities involved."

Dismay stole over her. More people meant more time wasted. "But that will take forever. We have to act quickly."

"Ms. Trent, a rash act at this point could get your niece killed. Surely you've heard the statistics. Most kidnapped children never make it back home alive." His face became serious. "This man has already killed once. If we don't want to provoke him, we need to plan our next step very carefully."

The balloon of hope burst. Her arms dropped to her sides, weights of helplessness rendering them useless. Lizzie's fate had been taken out of her control and placed in the hands of bureaucrats and hostage negotiators.

Jack started to speak. "Detective Rollins, I think—"

The detective again held up a hand. "I'm not listening to another word here. If anyone has anything else to say, they can say it downtown."

An angry flush reddened Jack's face. His mouth shut with a snap.

The great despondency that crept over Susanna drained her reserves of strength. Rollins was right, she had heard the statistics, but who would ever have guessed her precious Lizzie would be one of them? She felt like an old woman moving toward the chair to pick up her purse. The detective's words reminded her of all the terrible things that happened to kidnapped children. She'd seen the pictures on milk cartons, had noted the years-old date the child had been reported missing and the artist's sketch of what she would look like now, years later. Some of them never made it to the milk cartons. Their bodies were found, dumped in an out-of-the-way place. And some of them simply disappeared, never to be heard from again. The purse seemed to weigh a ton when she strung the strap across her shoulder.

She turned, resigned to going downtown to sit through an endless rehashing of the events of the past two days. Preston and Judge Van Cleve were pulling on their coats. Alice stood near R.H., with Jack nearby. Rollins had stepped into a corner and was speaking softly into his cell phone. Probably letting someone at headquarters know they were coming. Jack whispered something in his father's ear. The older man looked up at him, startled. His gaze flickered toward the detective, and then he nodded.

Jack came to Susanna's side as Rollins finished his phone call. Before the man could close the cover, R.H. crossed the room and planted himself, hands on his hips, speaking in a loud voice.

"Detective Rollins, I must speak with you. Only take a minute. You can spare a minute, can't you?"

Jack put a hand on her back and whispered, "Let's go."

Surprised, Susanna allowed herself to be guided to the door by the gentle pressure of his hand. "Where are we going?"

Jack spoke aloud. "We're going to police headquarters, like the detective said." He awarded a broad smile to the uniformed officer as they left the room.

His voice sounded falsely cheerful. Susanna gave him a sharp glance, but didn't question him further. He guided her through the front door, where a cold wind had begun to blow. She hunched her shoulders as he led her toward his truck.

"Are we really going to headquarters?" she asked as he helped her step up into the cab.

"Nope."

He slammed the door. She watched as he rounded the front bumper, her attention on full alert. He had a plan.

She waited until he slid beneath the steering wheel and strapped on his seat belt before asking, "Then where are we going?"

"You didn't think we were going to sit around and do nothing, did you?" A grin twisted his features as he turned the key in the ignition. "We're going to find Lizzie."

Jack put the truck in gear and cut the steering wheel. The tires left the narrow driveway and inched onto Judge Van Cleve's frozen lawn to edge around Preston's vehicle. When he pulled from the driveway onto the road, the front door of the house was still shut. Later he'd thank his father for doing a good job of distracting Rollins while he and Susanna made their getaway.

Susanna's fingers gripped the center console. "Detective Rollins will be furious."

"You want to go back?" He took his foot off the gas.

Her answer came almost before he got the question out of his mouth. "No."

He accelerated again. "Me either. I tried to tell him, but he wouldn't listen. I can't stand the thought of sitting around a conference table at police headquarters, going over everything we've already told them, when I'm pretty sure I know where she is."

Wide eyes fixed on him. "You do?"

A few drops of sleet speckled the windshield. Jack switched on the defroster. "Lizzie gave us the clues herself. She said the mean man wouldn't let her ride the horsies, there's no Cartoon Network and she can have all the peppermints she wants."

Her face remained blank. "Those are clues?"

"Sure they are. Exactly the same way the judge's clues gave us the location of the tokens. All we have to do is figure out what Lizzie meant, and she'll lead us right to her."

He glanced in the mirror, half afraid he'd see police lights flashing behind him. They probably had about fifteen minutes before the police started looking for them. Rollins wouldn't miss them until he got downtown to headquarters. By then, they'd be out of town.

"I still don't understand," Susanna said.

Jack held the wheel with one hand and raised one finger. "First she said the man wouldn't let her pet the horsies. Why would she mention horses unless she'd seen some? And if she wanted to pet them, that probably means they were close enough that she thought she might be able to touch them if she were allowed. She wouldn't see horses off in the distance and want to pet them."

"Okay, that makes sense."

He lifted a second finger. "Next she said the television didn't have the Cartoon Network, only boring stuff."

A wry smile twisted her lips. "Cartoons are Lizzie's obsession. She'd watch the Cartoon Network 24/7 if I allowed her to."

"Cartoon Network is part of the cable company's basic package, and all satellite companies have it, too. So if the television she's watching only has *boring stuff,* that means it isn't hooked to cable or satellite. She's watching Saturday afternoon shows on free broadcast networks, surely boring to a three-year-old."

She considered that, then nodded. "Okay. Go on. What do the peppermint candies mean?"

Jack grinned at her. "That was the clincher. Did you know that horses love peppermints?"

"So she's on a horse farm?" Hope flared in her eyes, but in the next moment she sagged in the seat. "Jack, we're in central Kentucky. There are thousands of horse farms around this area."

"Ah, but how many have a television with no cable and a brand-new giant-size package of peppermints in the kitchen? I know, because I put it there myself to feed the horses in the next pasture."

Sleet fell in earnest now. He switched on the wipers and cranked the defroster fan on high to hold the fog at bay.

"You did?"

He nodded. "Richard wouldn't take her to his house. What if she were spotted? He wouldn't risk that. Instead, he'd take her someplace where they wouldn't be seen, preferably someplace isolated. My family owns property out in the country, off Camp Nelson Road. We use it for hunting and fishing. There's a hunting lodge there, and we have a little television set so my father can check the stock market report on the evening news." He gave her a meaningful look. "No cable. It has an antenna."

"And you have horses?"

"No, but the guy who owns the next property over keeps a few horses there. When they see me, they hang out by the fence in front of our lodge because they know I always keep peppermints for them. I haven't been there in a couple months, but last time I was, I took a big bag and left them in the kitchen."

Her fingers dug into the vinyl on the console. "And Richard knows where this lodge is?"

"He was there last November during deer season. Not only that, but my father keeps a spare set of keys at the office. Richard has access to them, and I'm pretty sure there's a key to our trailer on that ring, too."

His cell phone rang. He glanced at the clock on the dashboard. Seventeen minutes since they had left the judge's house.

"I have a feeling I know who that is," he told her. "Detective Rollins probably wants to know why we aren't downtown." He left the phone in his pocket.

Thirty seconds after his phone stopped ringing, hers began. She pulled it out of her purse and looked at the screen. "You're right."

A flash of guilt assaulted him. They were evading the police. Could you go to jail for that? Probably. He would gladly spend time in jail if it meant Lizzie's safe return, but what about Susanna? He'd never forgive himself if he got her locked up.

Even worse, what if this is a stupid move that gets Lizzie killed?

Was he trying so hard to be Susanna's hero that he was acting rashly?

Her phone stopped ringing, and his started again almost immediately.

"Maybe I should answer it and tell him where we're going."

"No!" She clutched the seat belt. "He'll order us to turn around, to let the police handle it. But they won't, Jack. They'll wait until they've had a hundred meetings and worked out a plan and called in hostage negotiators. Meanwhile, Lizzie is in the hands of a murderer."

The ringing stopped and before her phone could begin again, she turned it off and dropped it back in her purse.

Jack tore his gaze away from her pleading eyes. "Once we get there and see that I'm right, we'll have to call Rollins. We can't do anything to endanger Lizzie." *Or you.* "Agreed?"

Her nod was quick, eager. "Agreed. If we're already there, Detective Rollins will have to act. In the meantime we'll stand guard and make sure Richard doesn't leave with Lizzie before the police arrive."

Rollins wouldn't like having his hand forced. But if they verified that Richard was, indeed, holding Lizzie out at the hunting lodge, maybe that would buy them some brownie points. Maybe the surly detective wouldn't throw the book at them.

Jack breathed a relieved sigh when he turned onto the curvy country road that would take them to his family's property. No doubt Rollins had notified the police to be on the lookout for his truck, but they weren't likely to patrol down here.

Sleet formed a thin layer of ice on the dirty snow that lined the road, but so far hadn't begun to stick to the pavement. Even so, he slowed as he negotiated the steep curves that wound down toward the river. A wall of rock towered above them on the right, layers of giant icicles that wouldn't melt for months suspended from the jagged stony edges. On the left, the ground formed a sheer drop-off that plunged to the Kentucky River four hundred feet below.

Lord, please let me be right. Let them be there. And if they are, please show us what to do when we find them.

NINETEEN

When the truck pulled off the road, Susanna released her grip on the shoulder strap. That was the scariest road she'd ever seen. Narrow and steep, it seemed to have been carved out of a mountain of rock. How did people get up it in bad weather? Of course, she hadn't seen any houses for several miles, so maybe not many people lived down here. Maybe they just came to hunt and fish, like Jack. She peered at the area outside the truck. There were no buildings in sight, only woods. Though the trees were stripped bare for winter, they stood so close together she couldn't see twenty feet inside the tree line.

She turned toward Jack. "Where's your hunting lodge?"

"Up a little farther. It's a mile or so off the pavement." He peered over the steering wheel toward a bend in the road. "I don't think we should drive up there, though. A bright red truck is pretty easy to spot. We'll have to hike."

If it would help get Lizzie back, she'd walk all the way to the Pacific Ocean. "What are we waiting for?"

Sleet rained down on them when they exited the truck. The snow on the grass between the road and the woods wasn't deep, but Susanna's sneakers were soaked within four steps through the slushy stuff. She pulled her jacket tight around her neck and plowed after Jack.

Inside the trees, the snow was scarce. Instead, a thick bed of decaying wet leaves covered the ground. She picked her frozen feet up so as not to shuffle, and matched Jack's footsteps. No traffic noises marred the silence of the woods, no roaring engines or honking horns. The only sound Susanna could hear was the crunch of leaves beneath her feet and her own breath as it rasped in and out of her lungs.

The sky above the treetops was an angry mass of thick dark clouds, the sun hidden from view. When they first entered the woods, Susanna was aware that they were moving at an angle to the main road. Soon, though, she lost all sense of direction.

She quickstepped up to Jack's side. "Is it much farther?"

He shook his head, then put a finger to his lips and pointed. Ahead lay a thick stand of evergreens that made the ones surrounding her yard look like yearlings. Jack slowed as they approached, placing each step with exaggerated care. She mimicked his actions.

A half dozen of the shaggy, overgrown bushes stood close together to provide a perfect shield. Jack crept to the one on the edge and, keeping his body hidden behind the cover of its branches, peered around. With a hand, he motioned for her to join him.

Susanna looked where he indicated. They'd reached the edge of the woods, though a few slender tree trunks stood in spacious isolation in the clearing in front of her. Twenty yards away stood a building. Rough planks formed the walls, the corners crisscrossed the way she'd seen log cabins built. But this place was too big to be called a cabin. What had Jack called it? A hunting lodge. It looked to be easily twice the size of her house. Snow covered the steeply pitched roof. Behind it, a small barn backed up to the rear wall.

The lodge faced an open field. Trees also surrounded the field, as though a pasture had been carved into the woods. A plank fence marked this side of the field, and four horses stood close together a short distance away. Lizzie's horsies. A one-lane dirt path, nothing more than two strips of packed ground, ran the length of the fence. At the end of that path, not far from the front door of the lodge, a green Explorer was parked at an angle. From the grim set of Jack's jaw, she didn't think the vehicle belonged to his family.

"We were right. That's Richard's vehicle," he whispered as he pulled his phone out of his pocket and turned it off. "I don't want this ringing at the wrong time."

"Are you going up there?" She inclined her head toward the lodge.

He nodded. "Wait here. I'll be right back."

"No way." She folded her arms with a stubborn jerk. "I'm going, too."

He looked as though he might argue for a moment, but then reconsidered. "The blinds in the windows on this side are closed, so hopefully we won't be seen. I hope he isn't standing guard. Stay close."

At the idea of Lizzie's kidnapper standing guard, her heart seemed to climb into her throat, and its erratic beating stifled any words she might have voiced. She managed a nod. Jack's eyes moved as he scanned the area around the cabin, and then he dashed forward. Susanna left the cover of the evergreen and sprinted after him. By the time they covered the short distance, her breath came in noisy gulps that had nothing to do with exertion. Small clouds formed in front of her mouth. She pressed her back against the rough wood.

I've got to calm down. If I hyperventilate and pass out, then I won't be able to help Lizzie.

She clamped a hand over her mouth and forced herself to breathe through her nose. In slowly. Out slowly. In slowly. Out slowly.

Jack peered into her face. *You okay?* he mouthed.

She nodded.

He motioned around the corner with a finger, then placed it over his lips. They were going to sneak around the corner. Quietly. She nodded again to show him that she understood. He crouched and leaned to peer around the edge, then crept forward. Bent nearly double, Susanna followed.

Four windows looked out toward the pasture. Jack passed the first one and crouched down below the second. Susanna stayed back as he inched upward, his head tilted sideways, until his eye cleared the window's ledge. Her pulse pounded in her ears. After what seemed an eternity, he slowly lowered into a crouch again.

His eyes locked on hers, and he gave a single nod.

Susanna clapped her hand over her mouth again, this time to stifle a cry of joy. Lizzie was here. Thank goodness, she was here.

Jack motioned for her to look. Susanna crept close and imitated his movements, rising slowly until she could see inside.

The blinds on the window were opened at an angle. She peered through the slats into a medium-size room with walls of unfinished wood. A stone fireplace dominated the wall on the left, with a red fabric-covered sofa and chair angled around it. A man sat on the sofa, his face in profile. To the right, a television set sat on a stand in the corner.

Susanna bit back another cry at the sight of Lizzie, parked on a chair almost directly in front of the screen.

Oh, baby, you're okay!

She drank in the sight of her curly haired niece, whose attention was fixed on the screen. If only they could barge in right now and grab her. Surely the two of them could overpower the man on the couch. Or Jack could, while she snatched Lizzie.

The man on the couch heaved himself up. Susanna collapsed into a crouch, heart thundering against her rib cage. Was he coming to look out the window?

Beside him, Susanna jerked away from the window, wide-eyed panic on her face. Frantic gestures told Jack that something was going on inside. He started to rise up to take a look, but she grabbed the front of his jacket and jerked him back down, shaking her head. She cast a fearful glance upward at the window, then pressed her body as close to the cabin as she could. Richard must be at the window. Jack held himself motionless, not daring even to breathe lest the fog of his breath give them away.

After an eternity, he heard a man speak inside. The words weren't clear, but the timbre was exactly the same as the muffled voice on the phone. Richard's voice. He recognized it easily now. More importantly, the sound came from farther inside the room, not near the window. He pointed toward the stand of evergreens, and Susanna nodded. She crept to the corner of the lodge, then ran for the cover of the trees, Jack one step behind her.

When they reached safety behind the bushy green branches, they stood panting.

"She looked okay." Joy shone in Susanna's eyes. "Oh, Jack, at least we know she's alive and unharmed."

"Thank the Lord for that." He unzipped his jacket to

retrieve his cell phone from the inside pocket, where he'd stashed it earlier. "Time to call in the troops."

She stopped him with a hand on his arm. "Do we have to wait? Can't we go get her now?"

The pleading in her eyes almost convinced him. How could a man say no to a beautiful, desperate woman?

With an effort, he shook his head. "It's not safe."

"He doesn't look that big. I'm sure you're a lot stronger. You could delay him while I grab Lizzie and run. Then we'll call the police to come get him and take him to jail."

Jack's resolve wavered. Richard wasn't a large man. Medium height, slender build. As far as Jack knew, he never saw the inside of a gym. Jack probably outweighed him by twenty pounds of muscle, thanks to his hours at the gym.

But Richard had managed to overpower Tom Ingram. True, Ingram had been strangled from behind, so Richard probably had the advantage of surprise. Still, could he risk Lizzie's safety on *probably?*

"We can't do anything else on our own, Susanna. Do you want to take a chance that Lizzie will get hurt?"

She hesitated only a moment, then her head drooped forward. "You're right."

He drew out the phone. "Like we said on the way here, now that we've found her Rollins will have to—"

A disturbance interrupted his sentence. The sound of hooves and the whinnying of horses. He crept to the end tree and peeked around. All four horses had run to the fence and stood in a row facing the lodge, their heads hanging over the top rail. The front door of the lodge was not visible from here, but obviously the horses had seen something.

Movement drew his attention. His gaze snapped toward a flash of pink and gold coming from the house. Lizzie, dressed in a fuzzy pink bathrobe and slippers covered the short distance to the fence, her attention fixed on the horses.

Not far behind her, Richard stepped into view. His voice carried clearly over the frozen ground. "Get in the car, kid. We don't have time to pet the horses."

If he got away with her, they might never see her again.

In a flash, Jack realized his mistake in leaving his truck parked up the road. Why hadn't he pulled it crosswise to block the dirt driveway? Then he would have cut off Richard's only escape route.

Beside him, Susanna had taken in the situation. She drew a raspy gasp, and in the next instant her scream pierced the air.

"Lizzie!"

Before Jack could stop her, she dashed from the cover of the trees and sprinted across the frozen ground, intent only on the golden-haired child who turned in surprise.

Apparently she didn't see the object that drew Jack's attention and sent an icy chill straight through to his core.

Richard's right hand clutched a pistol.

TWENTY

Lizzie turned toward Susanna, and a cry of delight tore from the child. "Susu! You came to get me." She opened her arms wide and ran forward.

From the corner of her eye, Susanna saw Richard stop, his head swivel in her direction, and then spring toward the child.

Oh, no, you don't.

She kicked into high speed, closed the distance and scooped up Lizzie. The joy of feeling those precious little arms around her neck again! She couldn't hesitate even a moment, though. Clasping the child in a tight embrace, she dashed toward the Explorer. If she could just get the vehicle between her and Richard, she could stall him with a cat-and-mouse game for the few seconds it would take for Jack to overpower him.

Her sneaker hit a patch of icy slush and threw her feet out from beneath her. She rolled to keep from falling on Lizzie, and landed flat on her back. Lizzie's head slammed down on her cheekbone, and stars exploded in her eyes. Her lungs, reeling from the impact, refused to cooperate for a minute, and she struggled for air. For a few seconds she was aware of nothing except a desperate need to breathe, and Lizzie's cries in her ears.

When her vision cleared, a terrifying sight swam into focus. Richard stood over her, the barrel of a gun pointed at her face.

"One more step and I'll pull the trigger."

The sound of movement behind her head suddenly ceased. She couldn't see Jack from this angle, but she knew he'd just skidded to a stop.

"Let them go, Richard."

Cold water from melting snow penetrated her clothing, but she didn't dare move. She held Lizzie's sobbing body tight and watched the face of the murderer standing over her.

"Jack." Richard's eyes narrowed, and he turned a scornful grimace toward her. "You didn't keep your word. I told you not to get anyone involved."

No, he'd told her not to call *the police,* but she held her tongue.

"So that's how you've managed to find two tokens so quickly." His gaze lifted. "I've always known you were no dummy, Jack, though it's beyond me why you stay in that dead-end job taking whatever meaningless assignments your father tosses your way."

"You can have the tokens," Jack said. "They're in my truck, just up the road. Leave Lizzie and Susanna here, and you and I will go get them right now."

A struggle crossed his features. "Your presence complicates things, doesn't it?" He looked down at Susanna. "If you told him, who else knows?"

She returned his gaze without blinking. "No one," she lied. "I needed help finding those tokens, so I called Jack. That's all."

"Hmm. Should I believe you?" He stared at her for a long moment, then took a step backward. "Get up. Let's go inside so I can think."

Lizzie's arms tightened even more around her neck as Susanna struggled to her feet. She risked a glance at Jack. He stood ten feet away, his hands clenched into fists at his side.

Richard thrust a hand beneath her arm and placed the gun's barrel at the side of her head. Cold metal bumped her temple and sent terror rippling through her body. He pushed her forward, toward the building.

"You, too, Jack," he said over his shoulder. "I can't leave you to go after the police. Keep your distance, though."

Susanna stepped across the threshold first, Richard close behind her. When they entered the room, Lizzie's cry turned into a wail.

"No! I don't want to go here again. I'm hungry."

"Shut up, kid. Have some more candy."

The child buried her face in Susanna's shoulder. "I don't want candy. I want macaroni and cheese."

"Shh. We'll get something to eat soon." Susanna pitched her voice to a soothing whisper. Hunger wasn't the only thing wrong with the poor child. Beneath the soft bathrobe, her little body trembled with the strain of the past few hours.

"Jack, take off your jacket and put it there." The gun swung away from her for a second as Richard gestured toward a corner. "Empty your pockets. I want your cell phone and the keys to your truck on the table."

A wave of despair nearly pulled her under. That cell phone was their only link to Detective Rollins, and help.

"I left my cell phone in the truck."

Susanna's ears perked up. She'd left hers in the truck, but Jack had brought his.

Disbelief colored Richard's features.

"Really," Jack insisted. "It's uncomfortable in my pocket when I drive, so I put it in the center console."

Richard studied him for a moment, then said, "Fine. Put everything else on the table."

Muscles bulged in Jack's cheeks as he clenched his jaw and obeyed. Susanna tried not to be obvious as she studied the pockets of his jeans for a telltale bulge of his cell phone. Nothing.

"Now pull that chair to the center of the room and sit in it."

Susanna watched as Jack dragged a wooden straight-back chair away from a small table in the corner. She searched his face for signs of confidence, of reason to hope. Instead, she saw only the desperation of their situation.

"Good." Richard looked at Susanna. "Now you. Put the kid down. Jacket off. Pockets empty."

Lizzie protested, but Susanna poured as much confidence into her voice as she could muster. "I'm not going anywhere, Lizzie. I'm just taking my coat off."

The child allowed herself to be lowered to the floor, but immediately wrapped her arms around Susanna's leg and hid her face against Susanna's thigh.

When she'd done as he said, the gun moved away from her head.

"You two sit there." He pointed toward the couch.

Susanna obeyed, and positioned herself at an angle against the arm, so she could see Jack's face at the opposite end of the small room.

When they were both out of arm's reach, Richard relaxed his grip on the gun. "If you'd done what you were supposed to, I wouldn't have hurt the girl, you know."

"The way you didn't hurt Mr. Ingram?" Her voice shot across the room like a poisonous dart.

Jack's eyes widened with an unspoken warning. She understood. *Don't upset the man with the gun.*

"I didn't intend to kill him. I just wanted to propose an arrangement, one that would be beneficial to both of us."

"An arrangement about those tokens?"

Richard turned toward Jack to answer. "Exactly. The same deal I have with R.H. They're worth a hundred thousand each, you know. I just wanted half for each one I recovered. I figured some of them out already, and would have gotten the rest, too. But to avoid suspicion they couldn't all be found by one person." Scorn twisted his lips. "Nobody would believe R.H. is that smart."

"But Mr. Ingram wouldn't agree." Susanna knew why. He'd already enlisted Justin's help in finding the tokens.

"Not only did he not agree, he threatened to expose me to the rest of the players." Fire leaped into Richard's eyes. "I couldn't allow that."

The look on his face sent a shaft of terror straight to Susanna's heart.

The gleam in Richard's eye alarmed Jack almost as much as his finger on the trigger of the gun. Before today he would not have thought Richard a madman, but that crazed, frantic glitter said otherwise. Maybe there was a shred of truth in his words, maybe he didn't set out to kill Ingram. He'd been desperate to avoid exposure, and resorted to murder in order to protect his own interests. And since then? Had the moment when Ingram's life slipped away beneath his hands tormented him? Surely murder would drive a man mad.

Lord, we need help.

Jack had to keep Richard talking until he could figure out what to do next. What about the tokens? Richard didn't know the Game had been exposed, or that Jack and Susanna knew any of the details.

"There are five tokens in my truck right now. That's two

hundred fifty thousand dollars, just waiting for you. Let us go and we won't say a word."

The man laughed. "Do you think I'm an idiot, Jack?"

"No, really. We'll stay here for however long you say, long enough for you to turn in the tokens to R.H. and collect your money. You can tie us up or whatever."

A smile crept over his face. "Now that's a good idea." He raised the gun and pointed it at Susanna's head. "In that storage room over there you'll find a coil of rope. Get it."

Jack's hopes sank as Susanna, with one unreadable look in his direction, obeyed. Lizzie stuck close to her side. When she returned, Richard jerked his head in Jack's direction.

"Tie his hands behind him. And don't try anything stupid, like leaving it loose. Loop the rope through the chair rails and pull it tight."

She came close, so close he could smell the sweet scent of her hair. Her pupils were black circles of fear that almost overtook the irises. He dipped into reserves of strength he didn't know he possessed and gave her a comforting smile. Hers trembled in response. When she stepped behind him, he dropped his hands around to the back of the chair and offered them to her.

As she worked, Richard spoke. "I'm sure you're smart enough to realize that R.H. won't simply hand me two hundred fifty thousand dollars in cash in return for those tokens. And when you three turn up missing, the Game will be off anyway. I'm afraid you've forced a change in my plans."

Missing?

A strangled sound escaped Susanna's throat.

Jack filled his voice with urgency. "Do whatever you want to me, but don't hurt them. Please." He wasn't above pleading in order to save Susanna and Lizzie.

"How chivalrous of you." Scorn curled Richard's lip. "Actually, I don't want to hurt anyone."

The rope pulled snug around Jack's wrists. "You don't?"

He leaned against the edge of the couch. "I never did. All I wanted was the money. You see, I've recently run afoul of some unsavory people who insist I owe them a rather large sum of money. If I don't pay, the results will be…" He grimaced. "Unpleasant."

One final tug on the rope binding his wrists and Susanna rose. Richard jerked the gun's barrel, motioning her to step away. She backed away, Lizzie still at her side, and stood in front of him.

"You're a gambler," Jack guessed.

Richard didn't bother to answer. He made a wide circle around him. "If the Game had paid off like I planned, I could have settled the debt. Still, I know the importance of diversification. Never risk everything on a single bet. I've made some arrangements, and have enough money socked away for a timely vanishing act."

Probably by embezzling it from Townsend Steak-houses.

Jack noted as Richard spoke, he'd circled directly behind the chair where Jack sat. Susanna's eyes had moved in a pale face as she followed him. She stood with her back to the door. Three steps and she could be through it. Jack didn't believe for a single second that Richard intended to let them go unharmed. He already faced murder and kidnapping charges. Why leave live, talking witnesses to testify against him if he were caught?

Jack turned his head just enough to see Richard's position. Could he thrust himself backward, chair and all? If he did, and it managed to catch Richard unaware, it might give Susanna a chance to make a break for it.

A movement behind him. Susanna gasped at the exact moment Jack identified the motion. Richard had raised the pistol high.

Pain exploded in the back of his head, and Jack slumped forward.

TWENTY-ONE

When the pistol crashed into Jack's head, Lizzie began to shriek. Susanna could only stare, horrified, at Jack's motionless body.

"Stop that noise."

The volume of Richard's shout shocked Lizzie into silence. She shrank against Susanna's leg, the shrieks reduced to a pathetic whimper. Susanna pressed the child close, her gaze fixed on Jack. His chest rose and fell, which meant he was still alive. Thank goodness. A dark line of blood appeared at his temple and trickled down his face. Nausea roiled in Susanna's stomach. Jack was hurt, maybe critically, and she could do nothing.

Richard stooped and tugged on the rope that bound Jack's wrists. "Not a bad job." He made a few adjustments, then straightened. "Here's what's going to happen now. You're going into that storage room, and I'm going to lock you in."

She glanced at the room where she'd gotten the rope. It was small, dark and full of tackle boxes, fishing poles and orange hunting vests. Instead of a regular doorknob, the door closed with an old-fashioned metal latch. An open padlock dangled from the loop. Once in there, she and

Lizzie would be stuck until someone found them. How long would that take?

In the next instant, she realized what he meant. He wasn't going to kill them. He was going to lock them up and leave them here.

We're getting out of this alive after all.

"What about Jack?"

Richard spared a glance at Jack's slumped figure. "Probably has a concussion. He'll be okay in a few days."

Did people die from concussions? He needed medical attention now, not in a few days. She opened her mouth to plead for him, but Richard thrust the gun barrel within six inches of her face.

"Now."

She headed for the closet, Lizzie still whimpering at her side. The sooner this maniac left them alone, the better.

When she started across the threshold, he stopped her. "Not the kid. She's going with me."

Stunned, Susanna whirled. "No! Don't take her. Please."

With his free hand, Richard grabbed Lizzie's arm. The hand with the gun shoved Susanna backward. Her feet caught on a tackle box and, flailing for balance, she grasped a rack of fishing poles. Sharp pain stabbed into her palm. The next instant, everything went black as Richard pulled the door closed.

"Don't take her." She grappled in the dark, but could not find a door handle. Ignoring the pain where the fishhook had penetrated her skin, she beat on the rough wood. "Please give her back."

"Listen to me." Richard's voice rose above Lizzie's screech. "In twenty-four hours, when I'm in the clear, I'll turn her loose in a public place. She'll tell them where you are. In the meantime, if you manage to get out of there, do nothing. If you set the police on me, I promise you that she'll end up just like Ingram. Do you believe me?"

The haunting image of Mr. Ingram's strangled body rose in her mind. A man who would kill one person would kill another. "Yes, I believe you."

"Good. Twenty-four hours. That's all I need."

Lizzie's cries of "Susu! Susu!" wrenched her heart. She heard a thud that sounded like a door closing, and Lizzie's voice faded. She pressed her ear against the door, straining to hear. The rough wood scraped the soft skin of her cheek. Then the only sound she heard was her own shuddering breath.

Lizzie was in the hands of a murderer once again.

"No!" Helpless desperation rose up in her. It wasn't fair. They'd come so close to rescuing Lizzie. Now she was gone, and Jack lay bound and injured in the next room. And there was nothing she could do. She was as helpless now as she had been when her mother and sister lay dying.

"It's not fair." She directed her scream toward the dark ceiling she could not see. Toward the God she could not see. "You could save her if You wanted to. Why won't You help us?"

Something scraped outside the door. She jerked upright and pushed her ear against the wood. "Jack?"

Silence, and then another scrape.

"Jack, is that you?"

A pause. "Yeah. Hold on a minute."

His words, weak but clear, penetrated the darkness that enshrouded her soul. A giddy light-headedness nearly knocked her off her feet.

More scraping noises sounded from the room outside her closet, and a couple of loud bangs. They came closer, until Jack's voice spoke again, this time from nearby.

"Get away from the door."

She fumbled in the darkness, pushing aside thick jackets and boxes, until she had wedged herself into a corner as far from the door as the small space allowed. "Okay."

The wall against which she huddled shook with the force of a mighty crash. And then another. And another.

The sound of splintering wood accompanied the fourth blow, and the final one broke through. The door swung open and light flooded the closet.

Susanna flew out and threw herself toward Jack. The chair to which he was still bound balanced on two legs, the back tilted against the far wall in the narrow hallway. He'd used the wedge as leverage to kick in the door.

She wrapped him in a ferocious hug, and when she pulled away, blood smeared the sleeves of her sweater.

"You're hurt."

"I'll be okay. Richard obviously isn't a professional thug. He stunned me, but I don't think it's serious. Just untie me and let's get out of here."

Susanna's fingers worked the tight knots. "He said we have to wait here for twenty-four hours."

"He can go jump in the river. We're not letting him get away with Lizzie."

The knots gave way, and she unwound the rope. "He's in a car. By the time we get to your truck, he'll be gone."

He stood, rubbing his wrists and grinning. "Who needs a truck?"

The determination on his face stirred a fierce sense of purpose inside her. They would get Lizzie back.

Jack rushed into the kitchen of the lodge, where they kept a set of keys tucked at the rear of a drawer. Hopefully Richard hadn't found them.

They were exactly where he'd left them.

He snatched them up and whirled to Susanna. "Go out

to the trees where we were hiding and find my cell phone. I dropped it when you took off after Lizzie. Call Rollins."

"Where are you going?"

He held up the keys. "To arrange our transportation."

With a nod, she shot out of the room. The front door slammed shut a second later. Jack unlocked the back door and headed outside to the shed. One of the best things about this property was the terrain—full of hills and paths and trails. Perfect for dirt-bike riding.

He unlocked the door of the shed and swung it open. The gloomy light cast a dim glow on a pair of motorcycles inside. He grabbed the handlebars of the closest one and wheeled it outside. Once clear of the shed, he swung his leg over, pushed the choke lever and stomped on the kickstarter. The engine sputtered.

Come on, come on. Start.

He planted his foot, rose up and stomped again. This time, the engine roared to life.

All right. Ready to roll.

When he rounded the corner of the house, Susanna stood beside the evergreens, talking into his phone. He zoomed across the frozen ground toward her. The rumble of the bike drowned out her words, but he heard her tone as she shouted a final word into the phone, then shoved it in her pocket.

"Detective Rollins isn't happy with us, but he's on his way," she yelled. Her eyes roamed over the bike. "I've never been on a motorcycle. What do I do?"

Jack grinned and scooted forward on the seat. "Climb on and hold tight."

He waited until she was in place, her arms wrapped snugly around his middle, then pulled back on the throttle. The bike shot forward. Once they found Richard, he had no idea how they'd get Lizzie back. There was still the not-so-small matter of the gun. But he'd deal with that when the time came. First, he had to catch up with that Explorer.

Frigid wind battered against her face as the motorcycle bounced over uneven ground. Susanna tightened her hold on Jack, using his body as a windscreen. Why hadn't she grabbed her jacket on the way out the door? If her limbs were numb with cold when they caught up with the Explorer, she wouldn't be able to help Lizzie.

Detective Rollins had been beyond furious when he answered her call. He'd launched into a tirade about withholding evidence and fleeing custody, but she'd cut him off. There had been no time for details. She had blurted out the bare facts, that Richard was escaping with Lizzie in a green Explorer, along with the location of the Townsend lodge. Hopefully her words made sense.

The motorcycle reached the main road. Sleet had left a thin layer of icy slush on the pavement. A set of fresh tire tracks formed a trail, a clear indicator of the direction Richard had taken. Instead of slowing for the turn, Jack accelerated. The motorcycle's tires bumped up onto the pavement with a jolt that jarred Susanna's teeth against each other. She clamped them together and peered over Jack's shoulder, trying to catch a glimpse of green.

The road wound up the mountain before them in steep, narrow curves. The rock face on the inside rose high into a storm-darkened sky. Susanna glanced to her right, down a rocky embankment. Slender tree trunks grew at an impossible angle. Bare branches stretched toward the sun like skeletal fingers grasping for food. Far below, Susanna glimpsed the swiftly moving waters of the Kentucky River.

The road curved, and she could see nothing beyond the next bend. Jack's wrist twisted on the handle grip, and the pitch of the motorcycle's engine rose as they picked up speed.

The bike's back tire slipped. A quick scream escaped Susanna's throat as Jack corrected. The pavement was littered with treacherous patches of ice. If they slid, they'd crash into the sheer rock wall on one side, or the metal guardrail on the other. Or worse, the bike would crash, but they'd be pitched over the side. Susanna buried her face in Jack's back, terrified to watch anymore.

Around the next curve, Jack tapped her leg. She opened her eyes and looked where he pointed. A stretch of the road ahead was visible from this angle. She glimpsed the green Explorer for a moment before it disappeared around a bend.

Hold on, Lizzie. We're coming.

They sped forward, and for a moment Susanna was so intent on spotting the fleeing vehicle that she forgot to be afraid. Then they were around the next curve, and she caught sight of it again. She strained at the windows, desperate for a glimpse of golden curls.

The back end of the Explorer swerved.

Brake lights flashed on.

The vehicle's rear slid inward, toward the rock, the front end toward the guardrail. Susanna watched, horrified, as the front bumper collided with the rail. A metallic crash echoed in her ears across the distance, louder even than the motorcycle's engine. The guardrail collapsed on impact. Metal screamed as it ripped apart, and the Explorer tumbled over the cliff.

TWENTY-TWO

Jack eased up on the throttle as they approached the crash site. Susanna's wail filled his ears, and her fingers dug into his flesh. Sick dread gnawed in his gut. Nobody could survive a plunge like that.

A patch of black ice winked with a deadly eye from the road six feet in front of the torn guardrail. He guided the bike to a stop in front of it. Susanna was off the back before he got the kickstand all the way down.

"Susanna, wait. Be careful."

He jumped from the bike and sprinted after her. Would she throw herself off the ledge after Lizzie? In the grips of grief and shock, she just might.

They reached the crash site at the same moment. Jack grabbed for her arm, ready to jerk her back if need be, but he shouldn't have worried. She stopped at the edge of the pavement, wide eyes fixed on a point below. One hand crept up to cover her mouth, and with the other, she pointed.

Jack looked over the edge. The Explorer was only twenty feet away. The back end tilted at a ninety-degree angle, the front pointing downward toward the river. Far below, muddy waters rushed with flash-flood intensity, the roar magnified by the surrounding ravine.

Another sound reached them. Screams. Lizzie's and Richard's.

"I'm going to get her." Susanna put a hand on the mangled guardrail and started forward.

"No, wait." Jack peered at the rocky ledge below them. He pasted on a fake-calm smile. "Did I ever tell you I'm an expert rock-climber?"

Suspicion filled her eyes. "You are?"

Does the climbing wall at the local game center count? "You bet." *Forgive me for the lie, Lord.*

He pulled her gently from the edge and stepped into her place. "Do you still have my phone?"

She nodded and fumbled in a pocket.

"Good. Call Rollins and tell him where we are. I'll be right back. With Lizzie."

Frantic hands grabbed at his shirt. "What can I do? I can't just stand here and do nothing."

His smile this time was real. "Now might be a good time to start praying again."

He dropped to his stomach and swung his legs over the edge.

With unsteady fingers, Susanna called Detective Rollins. Using curt words, she described the situation, then hung up without waiting for his response. That task done, she lowered herself to her knees and crawled to the pavement's edge.

The top of Jack's head was only a few feet below her. His descent was slow, deliberate, with long pauses between each step. Slivers of ice tapped against her back. The sleet had started again.

Jack said she should pray. Well, she was already on her knees.

God, please help him. Show him how to get down to her.

The prayer came in the form of a silent plea with the weight of desperation behind it. She'd already prayed twice today, though her angry shout in the closet might not count as a real prayer. Still, Jack had rescued her right afterward, hadn't he? A flicker of hope flared. Maybe God heard her after all.

Her next prayer wasn't silent.

"Please, God," she whispered. "She's only a little girl. I know You don't make deals, but I'll do anything. Just let Jack get her out of there safely."

As the words left her lips, the invisible bands constricting her chest seemed to loosen. Her breath came slightly, almost imperceptibly, easier.

Below her, Jack's hand reached for a branch. She heard a crack, and watched in terror as he slipped.

The branch broke off in Jack's right hand. The sudden shift of his weight jarred his foot from the tiny rock shelf where he'd planted it. He tightened his left-handed grip and scrabbled for a new handhold with his right. His fingers found an exposed root and, with a whispered prayer, he latched on.

The root held.

He paused to let his pulse slow to something resembling normal, then continued his descent.

After the first ten-foot drop, the embankment slanted at a forty-five-degree angle for the remainder of the plunge down to the river. Jagged rocks protruded from soil that had become muddy with sleet and snowmelt. Though every nerve in his body shouted for him to *hurry, hurry, hurry,* Jack forced himself to move slowly, deliberately. If he fell, Lizzie was a goner.

When he descended to a point parallel with the Explorer's back end, the reason for its sudden stop became clear. The frame on the driver's side rested on the tip of a rocky outcropping. On the side closest to Jack, a slender tree trunk had wedged beneath the axle. The weight of the vehicle strained against the muddy roots. Judging by the precarious placement of the rock, when the tree trunk gave, the vehicle would dislodge.

"Jack! Jack, help me!"

Richard's voice from inside the Explorer squealed with uncontrolled panic. Through the window Jack saw him twist in the driver's seat. When he did, the vehicle shifted with an audible ripping of roots from soil. Inside, both Lizzie and Richard screamed.

"Don't move." Jack pitched his voice high to be heard over their cries. "Stay completely still."

He climbed down the final few feet until he came parallel to the passenger window. Lizzie's tear-streaked face peered at him. In the driver's side, Richard's features were pinched with terror.

Jack found solid footing, then extended his neck to investigate the terrain in front of the Explorer. The slant became steeper, with few trees to break the fall between here and the riverbank.

"Move only your arm," he shouted at Richard, "and lower this window so we can hear each other better."

The passenger window glided downward. Lizzie's cries had become shuddering gulps. Jack schooled his features to smile at the child.

"Lizzie, you're being very good. You have to stay really still for a few minutes, okay?"

Her mouth trembled as she nodded.

Jack shifted his gaze to Richard. "The only thing holding you in place is a tree wedged in the rear axle. If you jostle it, the roots are going to give."

"Jack, don't leave me here." Terror showed plainly in Richard's eyes. "Please. I don't want to die."

Though he would never have thought it possible to feel compassion for a murderer and kidnapper, a wave of pity stirred inside Jack. "We've called for help. They'll be here in a minute. Just stay calm."

Jack glanced up to the road. The top of Susanna's blond head was just visible, her face hidden by a convex in the terrain. He saw no signs of flashing lights, heard no sirens. How long would it take Rollins to get a rescue team out here? Even five minutes might be too late.

Lord, I need some help here. Tell me what to do.

A breeze rattled the bare branches to his left. Jack gulped. This ravine formed a kind of wind tunnel. One more breeze like that could dislodge the vehicle and send both Lizzie and Richard to their deaths. If only there was some way to get them out now, but when Richard's one hundred sixty pounds moved, that was sure to shift the balance.

But Lizzie didn't weigh nearly that much.

An idea grabbed hold of his mind. He examined Lizzie's slender frame, her thin arms. How much did she weigh? Thirty pounds, maybe thirty-five?

He had to act fast.

"Lizzie, listen to me. I want you to move real slow and unbuckle your seat belt."

"What? No." Richard's screech spilled from the car. "She'll get us killed."

"No, she won't." Jack spoke with more confidence than he felt. *Lord, let it be the truth.* "As long as she doesn't make any sudden movements, she's light enough." He looked down at Lizzie. "Can you move real, real slow?"

"Y-yes."

Eyes wide, his body frozen in an unnatural statuelike pose, Richard wailed. With exaggerated slowness, Lizzie pressed the release button on her seat belt.

"Good girl." Jack shifted his feet to move closer to the door. He reached through the window and grabbed the front of the child's robe. He couldn't lift her out from this angle one-handed, but at least he had hold of her. "Now I want you to put your feet on the seat and stand up. Remember, you have to move very slowly."

Richard's wails continued as the child planted her feet on the seat and pushed upward. Jack supported her weight with his grip on the robe until she was almost fully standing and then he plucked her through the window. She wrapped her arms around his neck and he backed away to a safe distance from the vehicle.

A siren keened in the distance. He saw a flash of red reflecting off the rock face and tracked the progress of the vehicle as it rounded a curve on the road above.

"Richard, help is almost here. I'm going to get out of their way." A sturdy-looking tree grew a few feet to his left. He could anchor himself there and wait for the rescuers.

"No!" Richard's panicked howl echoed throughout the canyon. "You're going to leave me here."

He twisted in his seat, his hands fumbling with the seat belt. Metal creaked as the car shifted.

"No, I promise," Jack shouted. "Just stay still. They're right above you."

"You're lying!"

As Richard reached for the door handle, he leaned forward. The tree gave way with a loud crack. Jack watched, helpless, as the Explorer plunged down the ravine. It bumped over a jagged rock, flipped, and continued its journey in a roll. Richard's scream cut off abruptly. The descent ended when the vehicle landed, upside down, in the rushing, muddy waters.

Horrified, Jack watched the wheels spin helplessly in the air. He couldn't muster any satisfaction at Richard's death. He felt only pity for a life gone badly wrong.

Lizzie pressed her face into Jack's shoulder and started to cry.

"You're okay. It's over. We're going home."

He hugged her close and began the long climb up to reunite her and Susanna.

TWENTY-THREE

Emergency vehicles and police cruisers lined the steep curvy road. Helicopters soared overhead, one bearing police markings and the others with television logos emblazoned on their undersides. Jack ignored them all. He couldn't tear his gaze away from Susanna in the back of an ambulance. Lizzie had consented to the EMTs' request to examine her, but refused to let go of her Susu.

Susanna's hair was disheveled, her clothes streaked with dirt. The skin beneath her eyes was red and puffy, and still she was the most beautiful woman he'd ever seen.

Her head swiveled and she found him watching her. The smile that lit her face sent a dizzying wave straight to his heart.

"I could still throw the book at you." Detective Rollins's voice slapped at him. "This could have had a very different ending, you know. A more tragic ending."

Jack forced his attention on the angry man in front of him. "Yes, sir. I know. I'm sorry." No sense trying to justify his actions now. Time to pay the price.

The detective's eyes narrowed. "Yes, well. At least the child's okay." His gaze switched to a point behind Jack. "How did you get down here?" he demanded. "The road's supposed to be closed."

Jack turned and to his surprise, caught sight of his father striding toward them.

R.H. stomped up and planted his feet in front of the detective, his expression daring anyone to remove him. "I told those knot heads up there that my son was down here, and nobody was going to stop me." He tilted his chin and glared through the lower part of his eyes. "Nobody did."

Jack bit back a grin at the look of consternation on Rollins's face. The detective turned away, muttering something about unmanageable citizens.

When he was gone, R.H. lowered his head. "The rest of them are still down at headquarters, but when the police told us what happened, I took Lawrence's car." He didn't meet Jack's gaze, but stared at the road in front of him. "You did a fine job rescuing that little girl, Jack. I'm proud of you."

Jack's jaw dropped open. To his recollection, he'd never heard those words from his father's lips.

"Thank you," he said. "And thanks also for distracting Rollins so we could get away."

R.H. waved a hand in dismissal. "Least I could do. I feel responsible for this whole thing. I've been a fool." He shook his head. "I can't believe how gullible I've been. Richard hooked me like a fish in a pond. But you blew his ploy wide-open. And our Game, too."

"Will there be any charges filed because of the game?"

"Nah. No laws have been broken, no taxes evaded. Yet." He grimaced. "We talked while we were down at the police station, and we've all decided to make sizable contributions to charity." His eyebrows rose. "Think that church of yours could use a hundred thousand dollars?"

Jack laughed. "I'm sure Pastor Rob can find something to do with the money." His gaze strayed back to the ambulance. Someone had wrapped a blanket around Susanna's shoulders. She cradled Lizzie, rocking back and forth.

He looked at his father. "So, you and Alice, huh?"

R.H. shoved his hands in his pockets and shifted his weight from one foot to the other. "She's a fine woman. Puts up with a lot from me."

"I thought you always said women were a distraction."

"Well, a man can be wrong every now and then, can't he?" He straightened and looked Jack in the eye. "Seems I've been wrong about a lot of things lately. I'll try to do better."

Jack's mouth dropped open a second time. Was that actually an *apology?*

He was still trying to come up with a response when R.H. continued. "But you don't have to make the same mistakes I've made." With a deliberate gesture, he turned toward Susanna. "I think that one might be a keeper."

"You know what?" Jack clapped his father on the back before heading for the ambulance. "I think you're right."

Lizzie had finally fallen asleep in Susanna's arms. The EMT had pronounced her healthy, but they still needed to go to the hospital for a thorough checkup. Susanna shifted her from one shoulder to the other and arranged the blanket around the child's shoulders.

Thank You, God.

Would she ever stop whispering prayers of gratitude? No. Now that she'd started praying again, nothing would prevent her from continuing.

Outside the ambulance, red and blue lights flashed in the deepening darkness. Jack stood a little way off, talking to his father. R. H. Townsend's face had lost some of its arrogance in the hours since his blustering entrance at

Judge Van Cleve's home. Did that mean a softening toward his son? For Jack's sake, she hoped so.

Maybe God had arranged more than one reunion today.

Jack clapped his father on the back and headed toward her, his gaze fixed on her face. At the look in his eyes, warm joy settled deep inside her.

He stood at the ambulance's rear entrance and nodded toward Lizzie. "How's she doing?"

"She's fine, thank heavens." Susanna shook her head and corrected herself. "No. Thank God." She adjusted the blanket around Lizzie. "The past few days have taught me something. I've been wrong for a long time. About more than one thing."

She risked an upward glance, and her gaze was caught in his. Her fluttering heart skipped lightly, like a laughing child at play.

"Jack, how can I ever thank you?"

He didn't answer at first. Instead, he climbed into the ambulance and slid onto the stretcher beside her. His hand rose, and his finger came up to trace the outline of her cheek.

"You don't have to. I already know." The words came out in a husky whisper. "Words aren't necessary between—" his throat moved "—two people who love each other."

Emotion swelled from Susanna's heart to blur her vision.

Sometime during this ordeal, she had placed her trust in a rich man's son. But this time her trust was not misplaced. He was nothing like the man who had destroyed her life. Her heart was safe in Jack's care.

"I love you, too." The words tumbled from her lips in the second before Jack's kiss rendered speech impossible.

EPILOGUE

A handful of people sat in the first two rows in the church sanctuary that had become Susanna's church home. She entered and scanned the room, looking for her groom.

"There you are." He stood up from a chair on the front row, and lowered a cell phone from his ear. "I've been trying to call you, but your cell phone is turned off."

"Jack!" Lizzie dropped her hand and ran down the aisle.

Jack scooped her up in his arms. Susanna swallowed back a swell of joy. Finally, Lizzie had a daddy who cared about her. She blinked back tears. No crying, or she'd spoil her makeup. Was there a happier bride in the entire world?

She rushed forward to meet him halfway. "I'm sorry we're late. We had a little wardrobe difficulty."

"I spilled chocolate milk on my new dress," Lizzie told him, "so I hafta wear this old one."

Jack set her on the floor and held her at arm's length. "Well, I think you look beautiful." Appreciation gleamed in his eyes when his gaze swept Susanna's simple white dress. "And you look incredible."

From the front of the sanctuary, Pastor Rob called to

them. "So are we doing a wedding today or have you two changed your minds?"

Susanna grinned at Jack. "Not a chance."

"Then what are we waiting for?" Rob nodded toward his wife, who took her place behind the piano and began playing the classical piece Susanna had selected.

They arranged themselves with Lizzie between them and walked the rest of the way down the aisle together. Not a bridal procession, exactly, but this ceremony was everything Susanna had envisioned for the past year, since she realized she wanted to spend the rest of her life as Jack's wife. No extravagant, fancy ceremony for her. Just the three of them, together with a few close friends, celebrating the beginning of their new life.

When they reached the altar, their witnesses rose to stand with them. Susanna smiled her thanks as Alice, herself a bride of only a few months, handed her a simple bouquet of white roses. R.H. winked at Lizzie, who giggled, and took his place beside Jack. Marriage had done wonders for her soon-to-be father-in-law. Who would have thought a year ago that R. H. Townsend would be preparing to hand the reins of his empire over to his son? Or that he would become a doting grandfather to Lizzie? More prayers answered.

The music ended, and Pastor Rob leaned toward Susanna to speak in an undertone. "You know it's only because of me that Jack managed to snag you. I prayed him into it. On his own, this guy doesn't have a clue about women."

Susanna cut her eyes sideways at Jack. The grin he gave her set her insides tingling.

"Trust me, Pastor," she whispered. "He figured out this clue all by himself."

* * * * *

Dear Reader,

My husband says I have a devious mind. I'm always looking for a hidden motive, something that can be turned into a book. One day while watching a televised car auction, the price of a Corvette climbed to what I considered a ridiculous amount. Why would anyone pay that much money for a car? A thought occurred to me. What if he wasn't after the car at all? An auction would be a terrific way to transfer a hidden article from one person to another without others knowing. Of course, the buyer would run the risk of being outbid, so he'd have to be rich enough to pay whatever price the car commanded.

What would be worth such an outrageous price? I'd already written a book about hidden money *(Bluegrass Peril)* and hidden drugs *(Scent of Murder)*, so I didn't want to repeat those. What if the article didn't have any recognizable value? Something that, if found by the wrong person, wouldn't incriminate the buyer or the seller? Hmm…

I grabbed a pen and began jotting notes for the story that would become *A Deadly Game*. The idea expanded into one of the most fun books I've written. You should have seen me running around central Kentucky looking for places to hide tokens. Yep. A devious mind.

I hope you'll let me know what you thought of my book. Contact me through www.VirginiaSmith.org or become my friend on Facebook!

Virginia Smith

QUESTIONS FOR DISCUSSION

1. Jack and Susanna meet at a car auction before the opening of the book. What brings them together?

2. Because of her past experience, Susanna is reluctant to encourage Jack in any sort of relationship, especially a romantic one. What is she afraid of? How does Jack overcome her fears?

3. Jack refers to his father as R.H., even in his own thoughts. Why?

4. After the car trailer is broken into, Susanna barricades herself and Lizzie in the house by wedging chairs under the door handles. What else could she have done to prevent the kidnapping?

5. Why doesn't Jack want to ask Susanna on a date? What happens to change his mind?

6. Susanna doesn't trust the police. Are her fears justified? How does her distrust of Rollins affect her goal to rescue Lizzie?

7. Susanna honors Mr. Ingram's request to *tell no one* about the tokens. Why is she so loyal to her deceased boss? Was her loyalty misplaced?

8. Why does Jack feel uncomfortable in his father's home?

9. Susanna has honored her sister's wishes and not made Lizzie's father aware of her existence. Was that the right thing to do?

10. What makes Jack suspect that his father is involved in Lizzie's kidnapping?

11. As the story progressed, who did you pinpoint as a suspect, and why?

12. Susanna hasn't prayed in years. Why, and what happens to make her start praying again?

13. Which set of clues did you enjoy watching Jack and Susanna solve the most?

14. Jack has little respect for his father's business dealings and personal interactions, and yet he loves R.H. In what ways does Jack try to gain his father's approval?

15. Did you learn anything while reading *A Deadly Game* that you didn't know?

Love Inspired®
SUSPENSE

TITLES AVAILABLE NEXT MONTH
Available March 8, 2011

LISCNM0211

REQUEST YOUR FREE BOOKS!

2 FREE RIVETING INSPIRATIONAL NOVELS
PLUS 2 FREE MYSTERY GIFTS

YES! Please send me 2 FREE Love Inspired® Suspense novels and my 2 FREE mystery gifts (gifts are worth about $10). After receiving them, if I don't wish to receive any more books, I can return the shipping statement marked "cancel". If I don't cancel, I will receive 4 brand-new novels every month and be billed just $4.24 per book in the U.S. or $4.74 per book in Canada. That's a saving of at least 23% off the cover price. It's quite a bargain! Shipping and handling is just 50¢ per book in the U.S. and 75¢ per book in Canada.* I understand that accepting the 2 free books and gifts places me under no obligation to buy anything. I can always return a shipment and cancel at any time. Even if I never buy another book, the two free books and gifts are mine to keep forever.

123/323 IDN FDCT

Name	(PLEASE PRINT)	

Address		Apt. #

City	State/Prov.	Zip/Postal Code

Signature (if under 18, a parent or guardian must sign)

Mail to the Reader Service:
IN U.S.A.: P.O. Box 1867, Buffalo, NY 14240-1867
IN CANADA: P.O. Box 609, Fort Erie, Ontario L2A 5X3

Not valid for current subscribers to Love Inspired Suspense books.

**Are you a subscriber to Love Inspired Suspense
and want to receive the larger-print edition?
Call 1-800-873-8635 or visit www.ReaderService.com.**

* Terms and prices subject to change without notice. Prices do not include applicable taxes. Sales tax applicable in N.Y. Canadian residents will be charged applicable taxes. Offer not valid in Quebec. This offer is limited to one order per household. All orders subject to credit approval. Credit or debit balances in a customer's account(s) may be offset by any other outstanding balance owed by or to the customer. Please allow 4 to 6 weeks for delivery. Offer available while quantities last.

Your Privacy—The Reader Service is committed to protecting your privacy. Our Privacy Policy is available online at www.ReaderService.com or upon request from the Reader Service.

We make a portion of our mailing list available to reputable third parties that offer products we believe may interest you. If you prefer that we not exchange your name with third parties, or if you wish to clarify or modify your communication preferences, please visit us at www.ReaderService.com/consumerschoice or write to us at Reader Service Preference Service, P.O. Box 9062, Buffalo, NY 14269. Include your complete name and address.

Conor Russell knows what prairie living can do to a delicate female—that's why he's raising his daughter, Rachael, to be tough. But can the new schoolteacher, Virnie, look beyond his hard exterior and help both Conor and his daughter experience a family once and for all?

Find out in PRAIRIE COWBOY by Linda Ford, available March 2011 from Love Inspired Historical.

"You wanted to speak to me?" Virnie kept her voice admirably calm despite the way her insides vibrated at speaking to Conor, who had inadvertently opened an unwelcome door in her heart.

Conor seemed very interested in the reins draped across his palm. "I have to go to Gabe's farm and help him with his harvest. Rae can't go with me."

"Of course not. She has to attend school."

Conor's gaze rested on Rachael standing near the school watching them. He loved her so much it seemed to almost hurt him.

"I will miss her." His voice was low, edged with roughness. "But out here we do what has to be done without complaining."

She nodded, not understanding the warning note in his voice any more than she understood why she ached inside.

He jerked his gaze away as if aware of the tension lacing the air between them. "She needs someone to stay with her. Would you?"

Her mouth fell open. Was this God's answer for a way to spend more time with Rachael? He'd certainly found a unique way of doing it.

"Why, I'd love to stay with her. On one condition. You allow me to teach her a few skills around the house."

SHLIHEXP0311